"Why don't you kiss me?" she asked

"Because it won't stop," Aaron said.

"I know," Jenn replied, smiling.

Then his lips covered hers, and she could sense the frustration in his mouth, his tongue, in the way his fingers touched her face.

Her blood started to simmer, and the feel of his tongue inside her mouth, its furious demands, was the very best sort of pain. His hands fumbled, pulling her closer, her breasts to his torso, and her fingers tangled in the dark silk of his hair. Her phone, her prized phone, fell uselessly away, and once again Jenn was swept up in the very things that were bad.

Oh, but this. How could it be bad? He was whispering to her, using words that were neither pretty nor poetic, but the unfocused rasp in his voice and the hard pressure of his touch were hitting the spot right between her thighs.

It was all pleasure now. Apparently Mr. Wilderness Adventure had other ideas.

And soon she'd know what they were....

Blaze

Dear Reader,

This past summer, we went camping in a cabin in upstate New York. Tragically, there were many similarities to my heroine's accommodations in *Long Summer Nights*. But sometimes, against all odds, something miraculous happens. In my case, you manage to forget the fishhook you found in the mattress, and have a great time!

I hope you enjoy the romantic adventures of Aaron and Jennifer, and their quest for true love. I didn't intend to like Aaron as much as I did, but in the end he truly touched my heart.

Happy May!

Kathleen O'Reilly

Kathleen O'Reilly

LONG SUMMER NIGHTS

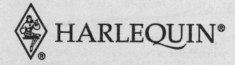

HARLEQUIN®

TORONTO • NEW YORK • LONDON
AMSTERDAM • PARIS • SYDNEY • HAMBURG
STOCKHOLM • ATHENS • TOKYO • MILAN • MADRID
PRAGUE • WARSAW • BUDAPEST • AUCKLAND

Recycling programs
for this product may
not exist in your area.

ISBN-13: 978-0-373-79545-1

LONG SUMMER NIGHTS

Copyright © 2010 by Kathleen Panov

This edition published by arrangement with Harlequin Books S.A.

For questions and comments about the quality of this book
please contact us at Customer_eCare@Harlequin.ca.

® and TM are trademarks of the publisher. Trademarks indicated with
® are registered in the United States Patent and Trademark Office, the
Canadian Trade Marks Office and in other countries.

www.eHarlequin.com

Printed in U.S.A.

ABOUT THE AUTHOR

Kathleen O'Reilly wrote her first romance at the age of eleven, which to her undying embarrassment was read aloud to her class. After taking more than twenty years to recover from the profound distress, she is now proud to finally announce her career—romance author. Now she is an award-winning author of nearly twenty romances published in countries all over the world. Kathleen lives in New York with her husband and their two children, who outwit her daily.

Books by Kathleen O'Reilly

HARLEQUIN BLAZE
297—BEYOND BREATHLESS*
309—BEYOND DARING*
321—BEYOND SEDUCTION*
382—SHAKEN AND STIRRED**
388—SEX, STRAIGHT UP**
394—NIGHTCAP**
485—HOT UNDER PRESSURE***
515—MIDNIGHT RESOLUTIONS***

*The Red Choo Diaries
**Those Sexy O'Sullivans
***Where You Least Expect It

1

THE TINY CABIN WAS A cobwebbed hovel. An abandoned relic left over from an era that predated air-conditioning and bed springs. Casually, coolly, completely in command, Jennifer Dade scanned the room. Yes, the cabin predated indoor plumbing, as well.

She glanced at the manager of the campgrounds, a tan, thirtysomething woman, who had lake-green eyes that seemed as weary and faded as the once-white apron she wore. Yet there remained a quiet dignity, as if she was not yet resigned to rejection. And no, it wasn't that Jenn wanted to be rejecter-girl and take her business elsewhere, but the *dirt...*

As if on cue, Jenn sneezed, and then met the woman's eyes. They were steady. Unflinching. Joan of Arc, prepared to be martyred at the stake.

Why now? Why this?

The place was borderline unlivable, and Jenn did have limits to what she'd put up with. She had standards. High standards. She thought of her last boyfriend, Taj, the twenty-four-year-old drummer with a love of the Cartoon Network. Mostly high standards.

The manager noticed her hesitation—understatement

of the year—and patted the head of the cherubic chubster who was clinging to her hip.

"You don't want to stay here, do you? You're here for the Summer Nights Festival, and you're expecting something a lot nicer, right? There's a bunch of bed-and-breakfasts up the road. The Wildrose Inn is the nicest, and I heard they had a cancellation. If you make it there before high tea, you might get in."

"The Wildrose Inn?" Jenn breathed the words, shallowly transported by the idea of a towering Victorian with rambling rosebushes that dotted the lawn. Tea on a silver platter…and a toilet. It sounded heavenly, with mass appeal. Commercial appeal. The sort of commercial appeal that would insure Jennifer's job.

The little girl piped in, flashing her big, blue Oliver Twist eyes and a grape-juice stain that extended from nose to chin. "It's all right, Momma. Somebody else will come soon. We'll find a renter. I know we will."

Watching the kid, Jenn felt something tug at her heart, and she wasn't sure if it was the first stirrings of maternal instincts—which frankly terrified her—or her stubborn impulse to drop a quarter in every panhandlers box, even though she knew it would only perpetuate the very impracticability of the homeless plight.

However, if she wanted to keep the job of her dreams, she needed to fight these urges. For the next two weeks, Jenn was on assignment, and her computer needed electricity. Ergo, if there was no electricity, there was no job.

So, even if she wanted to stay here, she couldn't. Problem solved.

She almost smiled until she noticed the black-plated plug in the wall. Okay, electricity was here.

Still, the readers would love the Wildrose Inn. Presidents had probably slept there. There was probably a charming love story about the ghosts that roamed the halls. Because of course, there would be ghosts at the Wildrose Inn. And a five-star chef who thrilled the critics.

The sad-faced kid began sucking her thumb. Jenn felt her womb contract, pulse, sigh. No. Be strong.

"It wasn't exactly what I had in mind. I was expecting something a little more…"

"Fancy," finished the woman, no stranger to the obvious.

Time for a new tactic, something that didn't make her feel like such a martyr-killer.

"This is the deluxe cabin?" asked Jennifer hopefully. Maybe the paper had made some clerical mishap, and Jenn had landed the supersaver accommodations instead? Times were tough; it was a possibility.

"My ex was a wilderness freak," the woman explained. "He loved the sounds and smells of nature, and bought this place for a song. Of course, then he leaves me to run it. Not that I want to talk bad about Emily's father—" she covered her daughters ears "—but if I called him an asshole, I'd offend thousands of butt cheeks everywhere."

Sorrowfully Jenn shook her head. "Been there, bagged that, sobbed at the ending. We're a gullible gender. Too softhearted to stand up for what is best for us. No, it's all about sacrifice, sacrifice, sacrifice."

It was a habit of Jenn's. Promote camaraderie, create intimacy, inspire trust. It was the key to her reporter's way, the secret to getting to the very heart of strangers in the span of sixty minutes or less.

But not this time. The woman heaved a self-sacrificing sigh, uncovered her daughter's ears, and then smoothed at nonexistent creases in her apron.

"You'll be happier at the Wildrose. It's really nice. They have these great down comforters, and in the afternoon,

Sven will do massages. His name isn't really Sven, it's actually Mario, but still, he has great hands."

Her apple cheeks blushed a dark scarlet, and Jennifer suspected the woman knew Mario's hands in the most intimate sort of way.

Sentimentality and guilt warred with her need to do this feature right, and Jenn glanced at the kid who was now milking this one for all it was worth, her grape-stained chin wobbling, her wide eyes brimming with tears.

It was like watching a little Meryl Streep, and Jenn had always been a sucker for Meryl Streep and her ability to convey heart-wrenching melancholy with only a quiet look. This kid had those same Oscar-winning genes in spades and knew it.

Unfortunately it wasn't completely an act.

Oh, hell.

Mind made up, Jennifer nodded. "I like this place. Sometimes I think it's important to get away from the distractions of the everyday world. A place where I can turn off the television."

"No television."

"And chuck the cell phone in the lake when the ringing gets too loud."

The woman laughed, a relieved laugh, and Jenn smiled to herself.

"Not a problem. No cell reception for miles."

Miles? *Miles?* Longingly Jenn stroked the new iPhone in her jean pocket, knowing she could never chuck it into the lake. All the hiking and nature apps that she'd loaded especially for this assignment? Pointless.

Techno-gadget lust versus the good of human kindness.

Her sigh was long and slightly overdramatized, but at

least now the manager looked calmer, and the kid looked more than a bit self-satisfied.

Yes. She was a sap, and for the next two weeks, she'd be a rustic, outdoorsy sap, and hopefully they didn't have poison ivy.

"Welcome to Harmony Springs. I'm Carolyn, and this is Emily."

Now that Jenn had made peace with her decision to abandon all the comforts of a postindustrialized society, she set her suitcase on the floor. "What do people do for bathrooms?"

Carolyn started to laugh. "We're not that rustic. There's a men's bath and ladies' bath right down the path. You won't be able to miss it, but it gets dark at night, so keep a flashlight handy. You brought your linens and soap, right?"

Sneaky Emily was watching her, daring her to back out of the deal now, not that Jenn was considering it—much. "Oh, yeah. I'm all set."

"Perfect. We'll get out of your hair. There's a movie every night in the main lodge, and a horseshoe tournament at dusk."

"Wow. I think I'm going to love this place," gushed Jennifer, and Carolyn smiled gratefully.

"You're a nice person."

"Sometimes. But I had an ex who dragged me on survivalist training for two weeks. I ended up with a sunburn and a bad case of poison ivy, and the pièce de résistance? He dumped me because I wasn't tough enough to hack it. I think I can make it fine." With or without three-ply toilet paper.

Really? Asked the snide little voice in her head.

"One last thing—we keep the grounds really quiet here. We only have two guests now, but Cabin Three really appreciates his privacy."

"He doesn't like children," muttered Emily, and Jenn kept her smile to herself. Obviously Cabin Three did not take kindly to having his emotions manipulated for capitalistic purposes.

"We don't know that, Emily," scolded her mother.

"Yes, we do. He tells me that all the time."

"I'll make sure to stay out of his way," Jenn assured them both, liking Cabin Three more and more.

Now that Emily's sales job was complete, the little girl threw open the wooden door, and dashed out of the cabin. She ran in unlaced sneakers, jumping down stairs and over rocks. Watching her unbridled freedom, Jenn envied that ability to run, laces whipping out wildly, uncaring of the consequences that might doom her to a bruised knee or, for example, losing the job of her dreams.

Before Carolyn could trail after her daughter, Jenn had one more thing she wanted to know. "Can I ask you something?" she asked.

Carolyn halted on the wooden porch and nodded, her eyes watching her child. It was always the loving mother who looked over the world with guarded eyes, wanting the best for their kids, wanting them to avoid the bumps and bruises of life. In that respect, Jenn's mother was exactly the same.

"Why don't you leave here if you're not happy?" she asked, not wanting to think about her overcautious parents at the moment.

Carolyn sucked in her lip, the way people do when they have an answer ready, but they know it's the wrong answer, so they chew on their mouth and their words, hoping to find a more socially acceptable way to spit it out. Almost all of the Dade family were notorious lip-suckers—except Jenn.

"I thought about leaving, about starting over, but not

yet. One day, I'm going to wake up and know that I'm ready, but right now, I wake up, and I go to work. Doing the cleaning and the laundry, running the movie, keeping Emily somewhat well-adjusted. That's enough for now. It makes me happy. It makes Emily happy, and if Emily is happy, then I'm happy."

"But don't you want more? Don't you feel like you're settling?" Jenn had an irrational fear of settling, of living her life on the terms as defined by Great American Societal Credo #32, A Woman Must be Successful and Recognized on Her Financial Merits, a well-trod treatise on the postfeminist era female.

"Why are you so interested?" Carolyn asked, obviously noting the not-so-well-disguised panic in Jenn's voice, which came as much from her own insecurities as it did from professional curiosity.

Jenn decided to come clean, because on a good day, she wasn't this edgy, but this wasn't a good day. It probably wouldn't be a good two weeks either, and although she didn't like to read the writing on the wall, sometimes it needed to be read.

"I'm a journalist. I'm here to write about this town, this place, the Summer Nights Festival, and I'm fighting for my job against a femme fatale who is sleeping with the boss. I don't have a chance in hell of keeping my job, but if I do, then my parents aren't right, and I'm twenty-seven years old, which is too old for my parents to be right, and so I have to come up with something here. Something fascinating. Something illuminating. Something mesmerizing. Something that will titillate my editor far more than the sight of Miss Nolita's naked garbanzos."

Carolyn knew desperation when she saw it. "You're sure you don't want to check out now? The Wildrose has this great chef. Four stars. In fact…"

Jenn held up a courageous hand.

"Let's forget about the chef for a minute. What would you do if you weren't here?"

"I don't let myself think that far ahead."

"Why not?"

"Because usually it's not good, and I like being happy. If I don't think too much about tomorrow, then I'm happy."

Most other female New Yorkers aspired to be dancers, or media captains, or heart-free mistresses to high-powered men. All Carolyn wanted was to be happy. Jenn made a mental note to investigate this self-satisfaction concept more fully. Women choosing happiness over the rigid expectations of the world? Story at eleven.

AARON BARKSDALE DRUMMED his fingers on the mahogany tabletop, glancing at his watch for the hundredth time, not wanting to look like an impatient male in a frilly, feminine world, but as a writer, he believed in absolute honestly, so yes, he was an impatient male in a frilly, feminine world.

But not impatient without cause. The elegant dining room of the Wildflower Inn was overstuffed with flowers, smothered by the rabid scents of hairspray...and *potpourri.*

Aaron hated potpourri. Neither was he especially fond of hacked-off flowers that were crammed into vases, and in his soul he knew that a woman's hair was best left soft and unshellacked. Feeling rather justified in his criticism, he leaned back in the pint-size chair and his fingers drummed even faster.

Where was Didi? She was always late, he reminded himself, but that didn't mean he had to like it.

"Excuse me. I don't mean to interrupt, but can you move your chair please?"

At the sound of a woman's voice, his fingers ceased

their drumming, and he turned to contemplate this newest irritation. Automatically his mouth curved into the politely expected smile, but it wasn't as difficult as usual.

She had soft brown eyes, possessing that wondrous sort of delight most commonly seen in magazine ads for cleaning products. Her face was long and thin, with a sharp nose well suited to intruding where it didn't belong. But she had nice hair, he admitted, only to be fair. Autumn gold waves that fell past her shoulders, soft and unshellacked—as it should be.

"Your chair?" she repeated in that same no-nonsense tone, and he reminded himself that people must be more dense in frilly, feminine worlds. Trying to oblige, he shifted an inch forward, until his knees lodged painfully against the adjacent chair. All social obligations now complete, he nodded to dismiss her.

"Do you need that much room?" asked the woman who would not be dismissed. "I'm trying to work," she offered as way of explanation, as if everyone chose a dining room as their personal office. Of course, with the hodgepodge of electronic gadgets spread on the table in front of her, he wasn't surprised she needed extra space.

"The chair's aren't that big," he argued, because if he moved any closer to the table, he'd be on top of it.

She looked him up and down, and smiled, patently fake. "You don't look fat."

Fat? Then he noticed the teasing look in her eyes. "Don't get nasty," he answered testily, because Aaron had never handled teasing well.

"I'm trying to work here, but I can't move my elbows. I need to move my elbows," she explained, flexing her arms over the small tabletop, her expression politely determined in that way of people who didn't know when to give up.

"Don't we all?" he muttered, before unhappily adjusting

his knees. Trying to block out the rest of the world, his fingers began nervously drumming once again.

She looked up, scowled at his hand.

"I'm making you unhappy, aren't I?" he asked, strangely happy about it.

As soon as he spoke, a heavily embalmed dowager at the next table shushed him. Obviously people in her world enjoyed the oozing scent of bad potpourri and didn't mind having their legs compressed in unnatural positions.

Cranky old biddy, he thought. Probably owned cats.

"Sorry," the younger woman apologized in a stage whisper, with a nod toward the next table. He nearly smiled when the older woman sniffed.

"It's not your fault," he told the younger woman magnanimously.

"I won't bother you again," she promised, but after that, he could still feel her staring at his back, and he told himself that the woman was very attractive, and he shouldn't mind having her stare at him. But this time, he could feel the tightness of his collar, the instinctive desire to cover his face. He told himself it was the surroundings, the filigreed trappings and overindulgence of gilt. When faced with too much noise, too much gold and too many eyes, he had an overwhelming urge to flee.

Finally he turned around, shuffling his chair sideways to face her. "I don't like being in crowds," he explained. "Especially fussy crowds with pearls and rose patterns and cucumber sandwiches." It was as close to an apology as he'd ever admitted.

"You don't get out much, do you?" she asked.

"Enough," he lied. He got out more than he wanted, and every time he did, he regretted the experience. When he got right to the point, as he knew he should, Aaron preferred isolation. He preferred the voices in his head, the world he created, the perfect turn of the phrase.

He preferred alone.

"Why are you here?" she asked, seeing through the lie.

"Lunch."

"Dragged the dragon out of his lair? Must be some friend."

He snickered at the thought. *Didi?* "She's not a friend."

"Oh," she replied, a wealth of innuendo in the word, and he choked back his laughter. She thought Didi was a date. "I'm sorry. I'll get back to work."

"Don't let me keep you from it," he said when she turned away, not bothering to correct her assumption.

Eventually she shifted again, knocking into his shoulders. "I can be a very bad procrastinator. Sometimes I'll know I should be working, but if I know I have the time, it's like pulling teeth."

"You should be more disciplined." Deciding that maybe she did need more room to work, he shifted to the other chair at the table. It was a little better. They weren't touching so much.

"Disciplined like you?" she asked with a mindful glance at his undisciplined fingers, and Aaron felt an odd heat on his face. A blush. Easily explained by the heat of the room, the presence of chemical additives and the disconcerting lack of oxygen.

"I never pretended to be a great example," he muttered, and before she turned away, she smiled.

There was a bleak trickle of sweat down his neck because he enjoyed her smile. It made him warm and lethargic, and Aaron didn't want to feel warm and lethargic, so he rubbed at his neck and concentrated on the Great Lily Massacre in the bud vase in the center of his table.

Not that it was enough. Out of the corner of his eye, he could observe her as the roller-ball pen scratched the well-thumbed pages of her Moleskin notebook. Careless and haphazard but energetic and slightly obsessed. He approved.

When she wrote, she talked to herself, reading aloud, and it wasn't half-bad. A few dangling participles. Some verbs that could have been punchier, but overall, it was decent. He got caught up watching the movement of her mouth, and decided that her mouth wasn't half-bad, either. It was fluid and expressive, never still, never concealing.

Oddly fascinated with her, Aaron forgot about the pungent smells and the cramped ache in his knees. It wasn't that she was pretty, but the light in her face drew him in. A hum of energy radiated about her, not relaxing, not comfortable, but always magnetic. When she was paused in her work, she would ruffle her hair, mussing it up even more. Each time she raised her hand, the dowager glared. Not liking the glares, Aaron gifted the dowager his best crocodile smile. Instantly the stares stopped.

The drama of the world played around the younger woman, but she was immune to it all. He didn't understand this ability to tune out the noises, and he wondered.

All too soon, the waiter came, presenting her with the check. As she pulled some cash from her overstuffed bag, she didn't look Aaron's way, and he told himself he was relieved. After all, he didn't like to be disturbed. But then she rose, and he found himself supremely disturbed. He didn't want to notice her, didn't want to leer at her body like some undersexed boy, but it was impossible. Truly. She had breasts that would make any man want her. High lush curves that would just fit his palms.

Beneath the table, his cock throbbed painfully, and he told himself that it had been too long since he'd had sex. At one shining moment in time, his sexual appetite had been legendary. It was humiliating to realize he'd been reduced to an ordinary man with ordinary tastes and a hard-on that could bisect a brick.

Needing to focus his energies elsewhere, his fingers drummed on the wooden tabletop, hard and fast, an eerily carnal rhythm.

Thank God no one was there to see.

Except for her.

As she walked away, she glanced at his drumming fingers and then smiled at him, a quick nervous smile, not a sexual invitation, not that his body knew the difference. Stupidly he stared—and of all the human foibles, Aaron hated stupidity most of all—but he couldn't help himself. For a second her eyes widened, zeroing in on him, cataloging each and every one of his human foibles, probably so she could pen them in her journal in her chicken-scratch scrawl.

Aaron looked hastily away. One innocent smile, and in his mind, he'd kissed her, stripped her and had her whispering his name between frenzied moans.

After she left, he calmed his oversexed blood and his undersexed cock, leaning back in his chair, breathing in the florid scent of rose like smelling salts.

In a few minutes, Aaron returned to his normally disagreeable state, and he smiled with relief, almost happy that Didi was late.

It was over an hour later when Didi finally showed, not that he should be surprised. There were many words to describe Didi Ziegler, *punctuality* not among them. She peered at the world through her owlish round glasses in a flamboyant red. People whispered that it was undiagnosed dementia to wear red past seventy. But Didi, who had broken hearts for nearly half a century, ignored the whispers and went airily on her way. And Aaron, who knew gossip to be only the most perverted form of the truth, chose to ignore them, as well.

"You're late," groused Aaron, obediently holding up his head as she kissed the air somewhere next to his ear.

"I like to see you squirm, darling. What sort of agent would I be if I didn't torture my client?"

"A humane one."

"You don't want a humane agent. You want a viper, and we both know it. Save the lies for your pages. Speaking of…" She raised her pencil-line brows until they disappeared into the silvery wisps of her crisply styled hair. "Do we have progress yet, or are you still twiddling your thumbs? I suppose twiddling is preferable to other, more colorful activities. But the isolation, the provincial wilderness…the mind assumes the worst."

Didi always knew the exact way to restore him back to equilibrium, and he flashed her a grateful smile. "Before you start the interrogation, I'd like to eat first. After the plates are cleared, we'll progress to pointless chitchat wherein you tell me all sorts of frothy drivel, and I'll pretend to care. Then I can complain about the state of the world, and the melting of the ice caps and ponder the fates of little baby seals."

She cocked back her head and laughed, a rich belly laugh that caused heads to turn, and Aaron's mouth twitched in amusement. "One of these days I will fire your worthless, delectable ass."

"I'm the client, Didi."

"And you keep bringing that up. A convenient truth that only muddies the patent unhealthiness of our business relationship."

"Bite me," he said with not a trace of malice.

"It's a good thing I don't have a full set of teeth, instead of these giant moons they call veneers. Tell me, Aaron, what happened to natural teeth, and natural boobs, and natural wrinkles? Ugly is a dying art form," she said, patting her beautifully coiffed hair slyly.

"You wear it well."

"If you call me Broom Hilda, you will die."

"You always look lovely." It was true. In his eyes, Didi represented the very best of the female sex. Razor-sharp, loyal, but with a large heart that few would ever see.

"I am not lovely, merely eccentric and egotistical. In the past, the men fell for it in droves."

"They still do," he said, and she beamed with approval.

After they ordered, they ate, and she dished the latest in the publishing world. Some old names, many new, and Aaron was glad he was longer a part of it. Moving north, "fleeing" as Didi termed it, had been the best decision of his life. Too bad she didn't see it that way.

"I saw your father."

"So?" he asked easily, shaking pepper over his plate, not really caring how much he used or where it landed.

"It was the Scribner dinner. He asked about you. He's getting old and scrawny, much like the rubber chicken you are condemning to your well-seasoned hell. He looked heartbroken, as well. I thought you would want to know."

"That's the Scotch."

"I could give him a message, although it would be a horrendous waste of my time and talents because I am not some plodding delivery service, especially when you could do it so easily yourself. However, because I am an exceptional agent, dedicated to my clients needs, I would. But only this once."

Aaron sawed at his chicken with excessive force. "Tell him the usual."

"It always makes me happy to spew vulgar obscenities and watch his eyes narrow to toothpicks. Martin is waiting for the manuscript," she added, daintily picking at her salad, turning from one unpleasant topic to another.

"I'm not ready to write again."

"Yes. I know. You are too emotionally frozen, devoid of all feeling and heart, and even worse, unable to plot your way out of a paper bag. Blah, blah, blah. You are becoming tedious."

He stared at her silently, as any self-respecting heartless, emotionally frozen man would do.

Unamused, she shot him a withering look.

"I need more time," he lied. Actually there were ten completed manuscripts under his bed. In fiction, Aaron believed in total honesty. In life, not so much.

"I've been telling him that for eight years. Eventually he will grow old and possibly die, and you will have squandered your opportunity. Not that I care."

Aaron shrugged, feeling the pecking bites of guilt, and he hated guilt. Guilt was usually directly followed by stupidity. "I'll have something when I have something." It was an empty promise, Didi knew it, and she moved aside the bud vase, the better to scowl at him.

"Show me what you have, Aaron. Give him a morsel, something to dangle in front of his greedy little eyes, and let them remember the vibrant talent that you are."

Aaron fought the urge to put the vase back in place and hide the disappointment in her eyes. "When I'm ready. The perfect book takes time. It's nearly impossible to do it twice in a lifetime."

"You will never be ready if you spend all your time in this dreary little ghost town. You should be in the city."

She spoke with all the arrogance of Aaron's father, some acquired from her two short years as Cecil Barksdale's mistress, but there was one important difference between the two—Didi actually looked at Aaron with affection. Aaron's father only looked in the mirror with affection. In the end, it was the same reason that both Didi and Aaron had left him.

"Since hell has now frozen and your will has fossilized into something large and beastly usually found in museums, I have no choice. For the next week, I will be slumming here for a short respite." She coughed, not so delicately. "If you feel a warm, relentless wind breathing down your neck, it will be me doing my job as I should be paid to do, if you were actually writing."

As he considered the horrific idea of someone sitting there, waiting for him, expecting to actual read his words, Aaron's fingers began to tap once again. His father had always said true genius could never be forced. There were few things that Aaron and Cecil agreed on. That was pretty much it.

He considered the lethal determination in Didi's face and knew that soon he would have to come clean. But not yet.

"Oh, you are the sly one," she murmured, her mouth curved in a Cheshire grin. "I know you've been writing. It's there in your face, your restless fingers." Delighted at his obvious misery, she rubbed her hands together. "There. I've decided. Every day we will have lunch, and you will report your progress."

"You can lunch wherever you choose. You'll lunch alone."

"You would treat me so shabbily, Aaron?" she asked, watching him with those piercing black eyes that knew him better than anyone.

"No," he said with a resigned sigh. With a single-minded efficiency, Aaron had chased away everyone in his life. Nine years later, it was only Didi who stuck beside him. He wasn't sure if it was his commission check that kept her in his life, or some stubborn desire to needle him to life. He suspected the later. Money had never been Didi's raison d'être.

"It would break my heart if you chose to brush me away now."

"You don't have a heart," he reminded her.

"True. But if I had a heart, it would break."

Aaron pushed at the chicken on his plate, seeing too much resemblance in himself and not proud of it. "As long as we don't eat here again," he told her, then swallowed a bite, doubts lodging in his throat like a bone. This was going to be a disaster and Didi's victorious smile didn't help.

Airily she waved her knife with as much skill as flair. "Of course, darling. Whatever you want."

2

"A QUIET TUESDAY NIGHT in Harmony Springs. Day One in this reporter's quest to find something interesting in this picturesque town where absolutely nothing ever happens. Did Quinn need to send me on this assignment? Do I have *sucker* stamped on my head? Do I need to keep asking these stupid rhetorical questions?"

Jenn clicked off the phone's voice recorder, and leaned back on the hard surface of the giant boulder. Above her was the night-dark sky. And stars. She'd heard the rumors of their existence. She'd seen pictures in books, but as a lifelong resident of New York, she'd never observed them in their natural habitat.

Out here in the solitary woods, there were other creatures in their natural habitat. She could hear them scuttling and slithering, and she told herself not to panic. Cute, furry things scuttled. Mouselike things. Mickey. Minnie. Mighty.

And then of course, there were the not-so-nice ones with devil-red eyes that glowed like the fires of hell. With large teeth that could chew on human flesh…and she could almost feel something crawling on her.

Instantly she brushed at her jeans and came away with

nothing but embarrassment. Sometimes an overactive imagination was a plus, and sometimes, like now, it was a definite problem. Taking a deep, focusing breath, she stood up, and held her phone to the moon like Excalibur.

Two bars. Almost enough to make a connection.

Standing on tiptoe, she reached for the stars.

At the sight of three magical bars, she squealed with delight, nearly dislodging her feet from terra firma.

Still, the near-death experience was worth it.

Her phone's display finally lit up, showing a map of the constellations above her head. Virgo and Centaurus. These were the twinkling constellations that were normally obliterated by the bright lights of the city. They seemed so low, so deceptively close, as if you could throw out your arms and touch them. It seemed that stars, much like New York politicians, were born to deceive.

She repeated the line in her head, liked it, and recorded it, a mental reminder of her literary prowess. And they thought journalists couldn't write.

Below her notes, the day's headlines crawled across the screen. All the things that happened in New York without her. A humbling experience, which proved that yes, the world did not revolve around Jenn.

But, her reporter's brain argued, wasn't that the whole point of being out here, at one with nature? It was a giant *screw you* to the concept of being at the center of everything. To say that you don't care. To say you don't need the rest of the world. To proclaim—a bit too loudly—that you're satisfied with only the company of me, myself and I.

Deciding the philosophical overtones weren't newsworthy, she sat down on the rock, reading over the day's headlines, getting distracted by the goat-rodeo they called Albany politics. She was deep into an op-ed piece on the latest budget referendum when she heard a new noise. Not scuttling, rustling. A large rustling, then a quiet oomph.

Not alone anymore. Quickly she closed her eyes in case the creatures had returned.

"Hello," drawled an annoyed voice. Not a mouse, she thought with relief, and opened her eyes, blinking twice in case her imagination had kicked in again.

No, not imagination. It was the uncooperative man from the inn. The same man who had dazzled her loins and piqued her curiosity. Yet no matter the pique or the dazzle, Jenn knew at a gut-deep level that this man would be another mistake.

His black hair was worn long, a man who didn't care about the opinion of the world. Tonight the cool blue eyes were arrogant and detached, missing the burning intensity of this afternoon. His nose was Romanesque, the profile of dictators and emperors and rulers. Nothing sensitive there. It was only the slight dimple in the center of his chin that made her wonder about the accuracy of her assessment.

But all those warning signs didn't mean she couldn't have fantasies, didn't remember the shot of excitement that chased through her this afternoon. The marvelous thing about dreams was that they were harmless, as long as you remembered they were only dreams.

Mr. Habitual Scowler sat down next to her, long legs stretched out in front of him, and she told herself there was nothing remotely dreamy about him.

"Your phone is very distracting," he said in a completely undreamy voice.

Surprised, Jenn looked at the innocent device in her hand. Yes, cell phone users were capable of many sins. Since she was intolerant of most of them, Jenn knew that both she was and her phone were being unjustly accused. "My phone?"

"I was trying to work, and I kept seeing this flash from my window. I told myself to ignore it, but I couldn't. So I walked over, looked out onto the normally darkened night sky, and I saw you sitting up here, performing some odd ritual."

"You could have ignored me," she pointed out.

"Yes, but then I kept telling myself that you might be some pagen worshipper, and might get naked and things went downhill from there. I couldn't work, and I needed to work, so I climbed up here to ask you to return to your cabin where you belong."

Immediately she realized who he was, and her heart bumped happily. Never a good sign. "You're in cabin number three, aren't you?"

"You've been spying on me?" he asked, sounding not as disturbed by that thought as most normal people would be.

"I don't spy," she said, defending herself. "I was warned not to disturb you."

"Too late. You've disturbed me." He pushed a hand through his hair, disturbing that, as well. It only added to his sexy quotient, and Jenn tried not to smile.

"I'm sure many mental health professionals would tell you that you were already disturbed long before I wandered onto this rock. And by the way, innocent rock-wandering would *not* be considered a disturbance by the population at large."

"At this campground, I'm the sole population at large. It's not a busy place."

"And now there's me. I'm looking at the stars, and I'm going to continue gazing at the stars, so if I'm disturbing you, I'm sorry, but I'm not going to stop."

"You're not gazing at the stars. You're gazing at your

phone. There's a perfectly good sky up there. You should try it."

"I don't know all the constellations. I'm learning. I suppose you know them all," she asked carefully. He didn't look like a romantic stargazer, she thought, not wanting anything else to add to his sexy quotient.

"No," he answered, and she sighed with relief. Although secretly she admitted that she liked the lack of fog in his eyes.

She pointed to the stars on her phone. "If you had a star app, you could learn them."

"Spoken like the commercially brainwashed American consumer that you are. Obsessed with convenience, purveyor of a thousand bits of minutia to manage an already hurried world. Devices that fool you into believing that you can rule time and have some control over your life. And in the end, those very things only make you a slave instead of the master."

Instinctively she knew it wouldn't be smart to laugh. If he hadn't sounded so completely sure of himself, she might have felt sorry for him. Instead, because perhaps there was a shred of uncomfortable truth, she crossed her arms over her chest and raised her brows in her best imitation of smug superiority. "This coming from a man who left his solitary cabin and climbed up on a rock, solely in hopes of a little gratuitous nudity? You're in no position to cast stones."

Sadly he didn't look the least bit ashamed. "I'm a mere man. Tethered to the weakness of the flesh and damned to experience life at its worst."

That was the problem with weakening flesh, she thought, wishing that *this time* her body could be a little smarter. Instead she was noticing the long, length of his thighs, the rangy breadth of his shoulders and the sexy way he looked at her when he didn't want to look at her. She'd never realized conflicted men could be so arousing.

"Who said that?" she asked.

"It's no one you'd ever heard of."

"He sounds overwrought."

"That's the polite term," he said, his teeth flashing in the dark, and she was shocked at how normal he looked. How appealing. How completely unromantic and yet still hot.

"Why are you here?" she asked, now completely over-wrought herself.

"Because I thought you were going to take off your clothes. I thought you would look nice without them."

Her eyes narrowed only because if he asked nicely, she might have considered. "You think that line will fool me? Leisure Suit Lothario doesn't come easy for you. In fact, you probably had to scrape the dregs of your social vo-cabulary to come up with that one. Ergo, the actual answer to my question is even worse than being branded a mere man."

As insults went, it was convoluted and scattered, mainly because her mind was still stuck back at taking off her clothes.

He looked at her sideways, his eyes amused. "What are you? Psychologist, or just nosy?"

"I'm a reporter."

At her words, the change in him was visible. The humor in his eyes faded, and his mouth tightened to a forbidding line. "Bottom-feeder."

Jenn was used to the lack of respect. As a journalist, she had trained herself to be immune. "You are a charmer. I bet your complimentary ways go over well with all the ladies. What do you have against reporters?"

"Do you want specifics, or are the broad, generalized sins of the species enough?"

"Specifics. I like dealing in truths."

"There is no truth, only whatever is convenient to whomever is speaking."

She didn't like his words, didn't like his bitterness, didn't like that he was correct. Since she was a kid she'd wanted to be a reporter, but she wasn't blind to the narrow line that a journalist had to walk. Integrity versus news.

Instinctively she changed the subject to something safer. Like sex. "Is this your idea of seduction? It's not working," she muttered, relieved when the tight smile appeared again.

"No. It's my idea of trying to get you off this rock."

He looked strangely content for a man who was disturbed, but she understood. He provoked her, but she could feel the answering thrum in her blood, the tightening of her skin, the brooding pulse between her thighs.

Frowning, she crossed her legs and his eyes followed the movement with a knowing awareness that didn't help the situation. "That didn't work with the pilgrims at Plymouth. It's not going to work with me. I have an assignment. I'm going to do my assignment, and I'm sorry if my presence disturbs your man-in-the-bubble existence. Actually, no, I'm not sorry. It's a lot of fun to irritate you."

He looked at her, his eyes a little too stunned. "Do you clip the wings off butterflies, as well?"

It was fascinating the way he drifted into insults so easily, using them like a shield, parrying anything that cut too close. "A butterfly, are we?" she said, raising a faux superior brow.

"I like to think in objectifying metaphors, dehumanizing as much as possible. It makes dealing with people much easier. Generally I like to avoid most people."

Not quite sure how to answer that one, not quite sure why he seemed content to sit with her on the rock, Jenn elected to remain silent, her legs firmly locked.

It was a beautiful night not to be thinking about sex. The sounds of nature weren't quite so forbidding when he was beside her. Somewhere an owl was hooting, and she realized she'd never heard the hoot of an owl. Crickets played and the stars shimmered in a velvet sky. When he didn't think she was looking, he would glance at the display on her phone, matching the constellation to the one's overhead. But she was always secretly looking, always watching him.

She liked him, she admitted. He was the best sort of man. Brutally honest and unafraid to speak his mind, dark and twisted such as it was. But it was that honesty that was refreshing.

He leaned back on the uneven surface of the stone, his chest rising steadily, his face turned up to the sky. He had a nice chest. He chose to hide it, much like he seemed to hide everything, a complete opposite of most of the other men she met who wanted to drone on about every aspect of their existence as if she couldn't wait to hang on each and every second of their day. Frankly a little mystery could be very sexy.

Maybe she should do this. Maybe she should have an affair. Maybe she should lean over four inches and kiss him. Feel that sharp mouth on hers. Slide her hands under the buttons of his shirt, and see if his heart would beat faster. At the moment, so deep into her own dreams, she thought that it would.

"What's your assignment?" he asked, which was the very worst question to ask while she was contemplating seduction.

Turning back to the matters at hand, which weren't

nearly as exciting as her current thoughts, she wiped sweaty palms on her jeans. "Harmony Springs. The Summer Nights Festival. The city-goers' annual mecca to a quiet upstate community that offers very little in comparison to the myriad wonders of the five boroughs, so why the heck do all these people come here?"

Perhaps he noted the snark in her voice. "Which do you work for? Fear-mongering scandal-chaser with a penchant for yellow journalism or overpriced glossies perpetuating an idea of beauty or wealth that no ordinary person could achieve?"

She looked at him sharply, surprised by the anger. These days people were cynical about government, business and international diplomacy. But the media had been defanged long ago.

"I work for a newspaper. Large. Manhattan-based. Many Pulitzers among the staff. You probably haven't heard of it."

Beneath the sarcasm, she still felt the thrill, the fierce pride in her job, which warred with her marginalized female propensity to remain humble. Usually the pride won out.

His mouth curved, and not in a happy way. "They give the Pulitzer to every journalistic rabble-rouser who spent their college years watching *All the President's Men*."

After all her bragging—completely deserved in her eyes—the man didn't look nearly as impressed as she'd hoped. Secretly she wanted to make that disdainful gaze flash with admiration and respect. Some of it was her own defensiveness, her own not quite deserved pride in her career. And some of it was because he belonged to the world of the intelligentsia and the literati. It was a nut she wanted to crack, a place she wanted to belong. At the paper, the halls were filled with people who dropped rhetorical devices at the drop of a hat. Instinctively she knew he lived in that high-brow existence, as well. His careful assessment of his surroundings, his use of language, his absolute moral certainty. So, who was he?

"I'm assuming you're not a reporter. What is your job?"

He waited a long time before replying. But eventually he met her eyes casually. Too casually. "Writer."

"Journalist?" she asked, not because she believed he was, but merely to see him dump all over the profession again. There was much to be gleaned from a person's prejudices.

"Fiction. Not so different."

A writer? Sure, there was something bohemian about him, but he seemed a little more intense than the unambitious dreamers who sat alone in their cave, waiting for the muse to come down and strike them with brilliance. No, this man would beat his muse senseless before he depended on someone else for his words.

He belonged somewhere else. Like Brooklyn, for instance.

"Why are you here?" she asked. "Why aren't you out among the teeming masses, mingling with the great unwashed dregs of humanity, obsessed with the eight million stories in the naked city?"

"Do you have to keep bringing up naked?"

He looked so upset at the idea of weakness, so worried that he was actually afflicted with something as common as lust, that Jenn wanted to shout childishly, "Naked, naked, naked," or perhaps, less childishly, to rip off her T-shirt and see what he'd do. Prudently she abstained from both and changed the subject.

"You're here to write? No, strike that. I still don't get

you. How you can stay here without going bonkers? Don't you want to know what's happening in the world?"

"Are people still getting robbed, are hurricanes still blowing, is the country still poised on the edge of ruin?"

Okay, he had a point, but it amazed her that anyone could stay so unplugged from the events of the world, the personalities, the happenings that affected them all. He didn't seem as though he'd be disinterested in the world. Maybe he didn't want to think that way, but she'd seen him watching her phone, she watched him at the inn earlier.

"But it's news," she protested, speaking out in defense of the American media institution. How could anyone ignore…everything?

"It's not news. It's old. Old as history, old as time."

"Old as sex," she contributed, noting the blush, pleased at his response.

"You promised," he protested. It was halfhearted, and his eyes warmed with lust and want, watching her the same way he watched everything else. Not liking it, not comfortable, but unable to stop.

"I didn't promise. You assumed," she answered, flirting dangerously, because she *didn't* want him to stop. She liked the want in his eyes, the way it made her heart pump with courage instead of fear. She liked the powerful heat in her blood.

Suddenly he was very close, a whisper's breath away. His legs were nearly brushing hers, the muscles in his arms tense with frustration. All she had to do was move one inch…

"Woman, you are the gate of Hell, the temptress of the forbidden tree. You are the first deserter of the divine law." The words were low and raw and she'd never felt so completely aroused in her life.

"Cecil, again?" she whispered, inching closer.

"No, Tertullian." His eyes met hers, fogged with desire. *For her.*

"Anytime," she whispered, feeling the curling tension inside her, the budded nipples straining against her T-shirt, begging for attention.

His astute gaze rested on her T-shirt, and his mouth strained as well, causing her nipples to harden in a completely Pavlovian manner.

"I should go," he announced, moving away from her, and she told herself she was glad. Relieved, even.

"The work is calling," she rationalized, trying to keep her mind focused on important things like her future career in journalism, instead of the length and width of his sexual prowess.

"Yes," he agreed, but he still wasn't leaving, and he showed very little intent of going so, and she could feel the panic growing inside her, in direct proportion to the needy urge to lean in a little closer, ease into that completely planned yet seemingly arbitrary moment when two lips collide.

Do not fall for this, she reminded herself. Ignore the sexy man with trouble simmering in his eyes. He wanted sex, his body nearly hummed from it, and unlike the twenty-four-year-old drummer with a passion for cartoons, this one would give her a night full of screaming orgasms, and then break her heart, most likely at the same time because he seemed to be that talented.

"Who are you?" she asked, thinking that if he was going to break her heart, she wanted to know his name.

"Aaron."

"Aaron who?"

"Smith."

"Really?" she drawled, not bothering to hide the sarcasm.

"It's actually Jenkins-Smith, but that seemed pretentious, so I just use Aaron Smith."

"Pleased to meet you, Mr. Smith. I'm Jennifer Dade, and from now on, I'll try to stay out of your way."

It was a desperate hint that *she* wasn't in his way, that he was sitting on *her* rock, and if he truly wanted all that solitude and privacy that he kept blustering about, then he'd have to act a little less…stimulated. Not that she was complaining. Much.

"I should go," he repeated, but he moved closer, and his eyes were on her mouth, and Jenn felt herself go hot, then cold. "Normally I like to ignore everyone else. It makes my life much more comfortable."

"Why can't you ignore me?" she asked, because she needed him to. She did not need this, but she couldn't ignore it. She couldn't ignore him.

He brushed a gentle finger across her brows. "You look at me with those busy eyes, always digging for your version of the truth, but grasping for the first clichéd insights into the psyche because it's easy and it makes your deadline, and it doesn't matter that there isn't always some three-point paragraph that explains who we are. You think there's always an answer, always a reason, but sometimes people are simply the way they are."

It was not what she wanted to hear, not what she had hoped to hear, and all those roiling emotions finally erupted. "And that's why you can't ignore me, because you just can't? The Twinkie defense? I had to be me. I was born to be bad. No, there's always a reason. You just don't want to tell me."

She thought he was going to leave. Thought she'd finally done it. Finally chased him away, but instead he looked with all the wretched want in his eyes. All the lonely hunger, combined with the same painful recklessness that she felt in herself.

"I wrote about you. This afternoon, I came home and spewed out reams of pages about someone with your face, your eyes, your hair."

"How did it end?" she asked, breathlessly tempted by the drama of it.

"You threw yourself in front of a train."

"Why?"

"You are the mariner's albatross, Ahab's white whale, the magnificent obsession. In the end, there was no alternative. You had to die," he said, sounding miserable and baffled.

But then his fingers reached out, touched her hand, such a small gesture, such a telling gestured. Sometimes sex was scratching an itch, and sometimes sex was the very human need to touch someone. All the phones, all the gadgets, all the machines in the world that mimicked human contact, and yet nothing came close to the absoluteness of sex.

"You like me, don't you?" she asked, twining her fingers through his, locking them there.

"I don't want to like you," he admitted. "You're very happy and sure of yourself and you like machines without souls."

"I don't want to like you either," she admitted, as well.

"But you do?" he asked. His eyes met hers, uncertain and unhappy and still hoping that she would say yes.

"Women don't like men like you," she said because she knew that unhappily hopeful was bad. Very, very bad. It spoke of vulnerabilities, and wounds, and manly suffering that had plagued women for thousands of years.

"What sort of man is that?"

If he were any other man, she'd have thought he was fishing, needing a stroke to his ego, but he didn't have those insecurities. Tragically like every other woman before her, she was falling for it in spades. "You want some three-point analysis that sums you up in fifty words or less?"

"Yes."

She chose the less dangerous answer. "You're brilliant and hurt and your writing draws you into humanity, but humanity repels you at the same time, and you can't reconcile those two aspects and it frustrates you."

"Do you know what frustrates me?" he asked.

"What?"

"How badly I want to kiss you. I hate your mouth. I love your mouth. When you talk all that blather, it's the sexiest thing I've ever heard."

"Why don't you kiss me?"

"Because it won't stop."

"I know," she said with a smile.

Then his lips covered hers, and she could feel the frustration in his mouth, his tongue, in the way his fingers anchored her face.

Her blood started to simmer and heat, and the feel of his tongue inside her mouth, and its furious demands, was the very best sort of pain. His hands fumbled, pulling her closer, her breasts to his torso, and her fingers tangled in the dark silk of his hair. Her phone, her prized phone, fell uselessly away, and once again Jenn was swept up in the very things that were bad.

Oh, but this. How could it be bad? He was whispering to her, using words that were neither pretty nor poetic, but the unfocused rasp in his voice, the hard pressure of his touch was hitting the spot right between her thighs.

Her shirt was open, and his mouth was on the thin silk of bra, licking and sucking, and telling her how tempting she was. The hungry pull was like shocks of electricity direct to her chest, and she heard her own moan. Impatiently he shoved the fabric aside, touching her, his mouth on her nipple once again, and Jenn was glad for the cover of darkness, for the cloud of the moon.

Mistakes I Made on Summer Vacation, Part VI. The One with the Great…

She reached for his fly, stroked him through the thick denim fabric. She knew there would be a Part VII, VIII and IX to the movie.

He thrust into her hand, and the movement was so marvelously wicked, so raw. Then he pulled at her own zipper, restless fingers sliding low between her panties, lower still. One finger flicked at her, long, insistent and aiming to please, and she stopped worrying, stopped thinking, focused on the pleasure.

The stars watched as he turned her, pulled her back against him, and she lay on him, his body cushioning her from the rock. His erection prodded her against her ass, and she wiggled against it, against him, but he stilled her, because apparently Mr. Wilderness Adventure had other ideas.

Soon she realized what they were.

His hands brushed her shirt off to the side, pulled at her bra until it hung off to one side, and then he slid her jeans low on her hips, and all her pertinent parts were exposed to the air. While his mouth nuzzled her neck, his hands roamed over her like an explorer and she was his map.

Once again his finger thrust inside her, plunging deep, slick with her desire. Her pelvis tilted up into his hand, and her ass rode against him, and it was exquisite.

"You see the sky," he whispered low in her ear, "the moon, the stars."

She opened her eyes, blinked the world into focus and whimpered a yes.

"You don't need a phone for this," he said, pushing into

her once again, and she wanted to laugh, but it was too hard to breathe, too talk, to do anything but ride with his hand.

Back and forth his busy finger slid over her slit, finding her clit, stroking there, circling there, her body weeping with delight. She bucked against him, feeling the hard ridge at her ass, and he moaned, but she was pinned against him, his hands keeping her down, and the hard torture continued.

He seemed to like watching her squirm, liked to hear her whine and complain. Part sadist, that's what he was, because his hand was destroying her. His movements were faster, and she could feel him grinding against her ass, which only infuriated her, but all she could think of was chasing the high, chasing the feeling, chasing the stars.

She closed her eyes, her body arching, and her hips tilted up, and he laughed at her, and she wanted to make him pay, but not right now.

Right now, she only wanted to…

Come.

There. Instantly her breathing resumed, and her body fell against him, sated and sleepy, and she wanted more. She wanted him inside her. She wanted this.

Morning-after regrets be damned. Hell, great sex would probably inspire her to write a better story. Snag the Pulitzer. Show Little Lizette exactly how it was done.

With ethics. With integrity. With the feel of a hard man thrusting inside her.

Happily she turned, attacked his mouth with all the excitement building inside her.

But then he pulled back. The man who was going to help her secure her job pulled away.

Bastard.

She was furious that he was able to stop. That he had

the discipline, the ability. And once again, she was left to find her focus.

Angry at him, at herself, at the way her jeans were unzipped, and her shirt was half torn, she stood and picked up her phone, because frankly, at the moment, she preferred it.

"I have a job. It's very important to me, and it depends on me pulling a rabbit out of a hat, and I don't even know if I can do it, but I have to try. If you sidetrack me, I will spend the next two weeks flat on my back, screaming my lungs out in orgasmic ecstasy. I don't need that. I have to spend the my time searching out whatever godforsaken newsworthy truths abound in these hills. I will not do this."

"You're right," he agreed easily, much more than she wanted. His eyes were shadowed in the dark, and she wished she could see them, wished she could see whether this was truth or a lie.

Not that she cared.

"I know I'm right. Now go," she told him because this was her rock. This was her place. He didn't want the stars or the night. He wanted his mangy cabin in the woods, so he could have it. But right now, he was going to have to prove to her that he could leave her. That he could leave the promise of sex, the promise of the human touch that she wanted to badly.

Slowly he got to his feet, the moon casting him in silver, and he shoved an unsteady hand through his hair. At that moment, she thought she had him. She thought he would admit defeat because he kept staring at her mouth, at her face, and his normally aloof eyes were still fogged with desire, and it was the most romantic thing she'd ever seen.

But in the end, he turned and swore, and she was alone on her rock, exactly as she'd asked.

After he disappeared, Jenn picked up her phone, prepared to get lost in the stars. Sadly after he had gone, the stars seemed to disappear, as well.

BACK IN HIS CABIN, Aaron pulled off his shirt, dragged off his jeans and stalked out to the lake. It was a rare moment when he yearned for the privacy of a cold shower. She had done this to him, and at the moment, the lake was all he had. The water was icy cold, enough to freeze a man's desire, diminish his libido.

Didn't work.

Shit.

Aaron lectured himself as he swam from one shore to the other, his arms stretching as far as they could. He didn't know anything about her. Only knew she was a reporter and that she was here to write the story of her life. A story, she so candidly admitted, about which she had no subject or no plan. No, she expected her story to hit her between her curious eyes, or perhaps, even more serendipitously, she wanted the damn story to squander itself between her creamy thighs like some sordid porn flick, exploding in his face like old history.

A reporter?

And stupid moron that he was, all he could do was flutter around her like a mindless moth, risking his existence for the light of the flame. He'd nearly cracked open his head, and did he stop touching her? Shouldn't he have been smart enough to walk away? Oh, hell no. Instead, *she* ended up being the one lecturing him on the problems of a liaison. Liaison. Such a pompous word for such a basic need. A man's insane compulsion to spend a moment with a woman in exchange for his soul.

His arms cut through the water, his legs pumping until

his muscles were on fire. Much smarter to work himself into exhaustion.

All he could think about was her splayed on the rock, nude, her arms reaching for him like some goddess of the earth. She, who worshipped at the altar of communication and technology, instead of the pleasures of the flesh.

Dammit.

The cold water was killer on his skin, completely useless on his dick. As he neared the shore of his cabin, Aaron dove under the water, then came up, before his feet settled on the unsteady shallows. He shook out his hair like a mongrel dog, and stalked toward the grass, feeling his head throb with every step and not caring. A concussion would be preferable to life-altering lust.

When he got to the dirt path, his still-tormented body stopped and turned to face the woman nearly hidden in the trees. Slim, with moonstruck hair and starlight eyes.

Aaron felt his body swell, his mouth dry, and he idiotically imagined that he could hear the shallow rasp of her breath.

His curse was loud and intended to chase her away, but she didn't move, as if she expected him to run to her, to plunder her, ludicrously believing that he was incapable of restraint.

In spite of everything he knew, every mistake he'd learned from, every calculated step that he prided himself on, still, *still* he wanted to taste her again, absorb her undaunted breath, and gulp in great, greedy gulps of her being. She, with the bright, eloquent eyes that desired him, that mocked him, that dared him.

Right, he assured himself, while his merry cock gave truth to the lie. Still lying to himself, still believing himself completely in command, he took one hungry step toward her, toward the siren's whisper of her allure, but then, because he wouldn't go back to that life, sanity resumed. He stopped himself, putting his well-tended restraint back firmly in its place.

Her swollen mouth curved, twitched, because she knew what it cost him to walk away. But no matter.

Soulless, heartless, he made his way back to his cabin, pride and self-control precisely back in place.

JENN STAGGERED BACK against the trunk of the nearest tree, because she needed to stay standing, and she needed to breathe.

She'd never seen a man more beautifully built, more perfectly arranged. He had no accordion abs sculpted from a love affair with weights. He had no bowling-ball biceps artfully crafted from tedious curls. No, he was lean and loose-limbed and heavily aroused.

Oh, that was the worst. He was thick and powerful, and she could feel him between her thighs, inside her, and she wanted that, wanted him.

She rubbed her arms, feeling the night breeze on her skin, warm and damp. The air had hovered around him, steamed with his desire.

In the city, men didn't want like that, they didn't ache with it. They didn't suffer with the very thought of it. Something out here stripped away the polish from the surface, or maybe it wasn't this place. Maybe it was only him.

Aaron.

She'd come to his cabin to apologize, at least that was the story she'd invented, but then she heard the sounds from the lake. Safe behind the cover of the trees, she watched him swim, watching all that untapped energy.

It was unnerving. It was arousing.

She was in such big trouble. Instinctively she knew he was a mistake. Yes, she'd had more than her share of them.

Even when she tried for safe and easy, it was still a mistake. For example, the senior financial analyst from Tribeca, with the great apartment and nervous smile. There was no women's magazine that would call him a Dating Don't—unless it was *Playgirl*. To the uneducated eye, he appeared completely normal and tending to boring. Two dates later she learned that the nervous smile was due to a compulsive tendency to shoplift. He'd stopped in a drugstore for aspirin, and she'd nearly been arrested in the process.

Oh, sure, the cop had been very nice and understanding with flirty eyes. In fact, the cop was so nice that he'd let Jenn off with only her promise to call him. If she hadn't been careful she wouldn't have noticed the wedding ring on his finger.

Jerk.

But the cop was different from the man she'd met today. Aaron wasn't flirty, wasn't fun and would never pretend. Hide, yes, but there was something that drew her to him….

Still not being smart, her eyes searched out cabin number three, nearly hidden in the woods, a dim light in the window. Not an invitation. Not even close. She heard a furious clacking sound, fingers attacking the typewriter keys.

A typewriter?

Unable to resist, she smiled.

The torture of it suited him, with no room for mistakes or edits. No. Whatever words he allowed on the page would have to be perfection.

Feeling far from perfection herself, she went back to her lonely cabin number five. There she pulled on her favorite T-shirt, falling back on her uncomfortable mattress, still feeling the hard fingers on her breast, the burn of his kiss.

That night, she didn't worry about mice or snakes. Instead she dreamed of a man with passion-fogged eyes.

3

THE NEXT MORNING, there were no garbage trucks, or honking cars, or the clangs and clanks of the city. This was an odd song. Musical. Cheerful.

Birds. Yes, that's what that sound was. For a second she lay there, listening, waiting for the noises to begin.

The quiet bothered her, the idea that she could hear the aimless rattles in her brain. The great thing about Manhattan was that it was impossible to feel aimless. There were always directions to be found if you were looking. Uptown, downtown, north and south. In the city, everyone always had a focus, always had a destination. But here, in Harmony Springs, it was easy to second-guess her own footloose life-navigational skills.

Like last night for instance? Making out on a rock with Mr. Dead Poets Society.

So why didn't it feel like a mistake? Why was she contemplating going back for more? Yes, that was the smoking orgasm talking there.

However, before there would be more orgasms, there needed to be focus, direction and actual pursuit of her assignment.

It would have been easier if there was coffee, but alas, in

her cabin there was none, no Starbucks, but her well-trained java-jazzed nose told her that somewhere in this veritable island of dystopia, coffee was brewing. Excellent coffee. Full-bodied, highly caffeinated. It wasn't long before she tracked the ambrosia to the campground office, where she found Carolyn hard at work, squinting at the computer monitor and muttering to herself.

"Fudge. Fudge. Floundering fudge."

"Problem?" asked Jenn politely, and felt guilty when Carolyn jumped.

"Sorry," Carolyn said, rubbing her neck. "You're very quiet."

"Not usually. What are you doing?" Casually, not meaning to pry, or actually not to look as though she was prying, she peeked at the screen. "What is that?"

"E-mail."

Now, that Jenn understood. The link with the outside world, the unbreakable bonds that connected the people of the planet. And judging by the screenful of messages, Carolyn had more messages than she did. Yes, it was petty to notice, but it didn't make it any less true. "You have a lot of friends," Jenn said casually, as if everybody had that many friends.

Carolyn laughed. "These aren't for me. It's for my boss."

Jenn smiled, because ha-ha, of course she'd known that nobody could have that many e-mail buddies. "Who's your boss? I thought you owned the campground?"

"No, I'm a virtual assistant."

"Wow, that's so cool. What do you have to do?" asked Jenn, wanting to know more, because at this point it was wise to consider all vocational options—in case she needed them later, for instance.

"Read e-mails, answer e-mails and manage finances."

"Do you have a lot of clients?" That many e-mails, that much stuff, that much obligation… It boggled the mind.

"Only one. He's a writer."

One? Wow. "So how'd you get the gig?"

"I get a referral from a friend. It keeps Emily in shoes."

Self-deprecating but also content. Jenn mulled the paradox.

"What about the rest of your family?" she asked, because an absent family could explain the disconnect. No hovering parents, no need to worry about excessive expectations.

Carolyn shrugged, sucked in her lip, and patiently Jenn waited for the answer. "Not so happy there. Dad, well, he wasn't exactly the picture of responsibility. Mom thought he had life insurance, he didn't. Left her with a mess of problems. I help out with what I can, but I guess good fiscal sense doesn't run in my gene pool."

"You don't seem upset."

"I don't let myself worry. It's self-destructive and Emily catches on and gets cranky."

"But don't you get mad at your dad?"

Carolyn cast her a sideways look. "Are you kidding? All the time. But you have to work past it."

Jenn couldn't compute that last part. Parents weren't supposed to be human and make mistakes. They were supposed to be all-knowing, all-loving and not capable of stupid judgment. "I think you're doing a helluva lot better than I would."

No hypocrisy there, because stuck out in the woods, living alone and surfing some other dude's e-mails, no, Jenn didn't have the strength.

"You'd be surprised. You don't know what you're capable of until you have to live through it. And it's not like

I'm some Nature Nanny. Sometimes I cuss, sometimes I drink a little too much wine, and sometimes…"

Jenn lifted a brow, nodded wisely. "Mario?"

Carolyn looked around, obviously searching for people who would cruelly judge her for perhaps being overly friendly with a man. Seeing no one in the room that had any business at all in even thinking such things, Carolyn bobbed her head once.

It was very hard being a woman of certain needs, i.e. not a robot.

Making herself at home, Jenn casually strolled to the coffeepot and poured herself a cup. "Don't you suffocate here sometimes? Everybody knows everybody. Everybody sees everybody. And if you and Mario or you and somebody else happen to hum-hum-hum-hum, then doesn't it bother you?"

Part of the question was curiosity, and part was the devious female mind that needed to know whether Carolyn and Aaron had ever…

Carolyn was nice, attractive, and Aaron was…very efficient in the art of the orgasm.

"Nobody knows," admitted Carolyn.

"Really?"

"Except for you."

"Telling the reporter all your most valuable secrets? Not very bright, are we?"

Carolyn snorted. "Not even on a good day."

Jenn took a sip and sighed as the hot joe warmed her throat and zapped her brain. "It's men. They make us stupid. So stupid."

"You got a guy back in the city?"

"No," Jenn scoffed.

Carolyn watched her curiously, and then enlightenment

flashed in her eyes "Oh." Then she frowned. Thought. Worried. "Seriously?"

Jenn flushed. "Not seriously. It was a moment."

"Really? I didn't think he had moments."

"Have you tried?" asked Jenn carefully.

"Aaron?" She laughed. "Good God. No." Then she held up a hand. "Let us rephrase. He's my only constant renter. Money trumps all."

"He's lived here a long time?"

"Seven years."

"You haven't wondered?" It had taken Jenn one night to succumb to temptation. The idea of resisting for seven years seemed…impossible.

"No. I have a daughter. I can't be curious too close to home."

"Oh," murmured Jenn, trying to sound blasé, then gave up. "Do you think he's ever killed anyone?"

"Physically or does verbally count?"

"The criminal sort of death."

"No. All he does is stay in his cabin. Writes. Glowers."

"And don't you want to know his story?"

Gently, Carolyn removed the coffee cup from Jenn's hands and sat her down in a very maternal manner. "I can see this is going to be a problem for you, and let me tell you about this place. There are two kinds of people in Harmony Springs. The ones who grew up here and have chosen to stay. There's about four that fall into that category. And the rest are people who came here, usually on the road to somewhere else, but they like the idea of a hideaway where people didn't worry so much about where everyone came from, or what their story is."

"Am I going to have problems finding something to write about?"

"Probably."

"Why couldn't you have told me that on Day One, and sent me merrily on my way to someplace like Hollywood or Vegas, where everybody wants to tell their story?"

"There's a lot of dirt here, Jenn. You just got to know where to look."

"Where do I start?"

"Browse the shops on Main. Mr. Goodnight in the antique store will talk your ear off, most of it worthless, but who knows. And don't forget to stop in the ice-cream store."

"Ice cream? I love ice cream."

Carolyn only laughed.

WITH CAFFEINE-FUELED courage pumping through her veins, Jenn finally broke down and braved the need for personal hygiene, aka the community shower. And to be fair, as shower houses went, the ones at the campground were not half-bad. There was gloriously hot water. The concrete floor and walls were painted an antiseptic white, and scarlet poppies bloomed all over the shower curtain.

Privacy, cleanliness and functionality. In the middle of the room, a wooden bench provided a place for clothes or sitting, or whatever else people did in shower houses. Jenn wasn't sure, but the bench did provide a great dry spot for her things.

Yes, she had a certain *Psycho* moment when she stepped into the stall, but the hot water did a fab job of washing away dirt, dust and Jenn's general fear and loathing of the great outdoors. Honestly this wasn't so bad. Earlier she'd bought a bottle of tropical gardens shampoo at the store, and if she worked very hard, she could imagine herself in a lush green jungle, warm spring rain rushing over her body, exotic birds calling high among the branches, and there in the corner was Cabana Boy, awaiting with a warm towel.

Having been blessed with an active imagination, Cabana Boy soon morphed into fully grown, fully aroused, fully unhappy Cabana Man, who wouldn't have held a towel if his life depended on it.

If only he wasn't so dark and mysterious in those ways that mothers always warned. If only he wasn't so…large. Her body began to tingle and whirr, tiny currents of nerves that started with her breasts, moved lower to swirl between her thighs, finally gliding over her…

Toes?

Jenn glanced down and screamed.

AARON WAS HARD AT WORK on the thirty-seventh draft of page forty-two when he first heard the scream. At first he thought it was only in his head. Sometimes that happened when he got lost in his book, but he wasn't writing a murder mystery.

Realizing he should do the right thing, he rushed out the door, paused to listen, and then heard it again.

The screams were coming from the showers?

Aaron wasn't a Boy Scout—he didn't like being a Boy Scout—and as he ran toward the concrete building, he wasn't happy that he was acting like one, but screaming invoked a fairly universal response. And then there was the possibility—probability—that it could be the disturbing Jennifer Dade.

A split second later he was skidding inside the woman's bathhouse, but thankfully there was no blood on the floor, no intruder at all. Water was flowing, but the screaming had stopped. All he could see was a steam-filled room that looked quite normal and only one shower in use. Everything looked normal until he peeked underneath the edge of the curtain and found a happy grass snake curled up on the shower floor.

Unfortunately there was no sign of Jennifer's feet.

"Jennifer?" he asked casually.

"Aaron? Is that you?" came her voice from behind the curtain, more than a little tense.

"Are you in there?"

"Get it away."

"Where are you?"

"Wedged between the walls. Get. It. Away."

Aha. Now the snake's relative contentment made perfect sense. "It's a grass snake," he explained in his most patient voice, instinctively knowing that laughing would be bad.

"I. Don't. Care. It slimed across my feet."

"Slithered," he corrected, leaning against the concrete divider

"I don't care if it tap-danced. Get. It. Away."

"You don't mind if I see you…naked?" he asked, frowning at the snake that was now the cause of bigger problems, because anonymous fondling on a rock at midnight was one thing, but gazing in a shower in the daytime was intimate and personal.

"Listen, if somebody's going to leer at my lady bits, you beat out the snake. Are you happy?"

No, he wasn't happy. Today he was supposed to be focused on his work, and his mind was entirely too happy for a man who didn't like happy. However, this was the right thing to do, his luridly happy mind defended.

Slowly he took a deep breath, reminding himself that in just a moment he would be back at the keys, typing. His hand pulled back the curtain, and even then he wasn't prepared for the shock to the gut.

Yes, there was shower-soaked Jenn, wedged between the two walls. Her feet were braced on one wall, her back braced on the other, but it was the in-between that caused him to bite down on his tongue.

It had been a long time since he'd seen a naked woman, he told himself in way of explanation. Ten hours in fact, which felt like four lifetimes. And last night she hadn't been completely naked, he mentally added. Why, she'd been cloaked in shadows and the clothes. Of course he hadn't gotten a good look at her. In light of all that, a bleeding tongue was perfectly understandable since last night he hadn't been exposed to the sparkling gleam of wet flesh, or the rosy bloom of a bare breast, or the damp triangle that beckons from between a woman's thighs.

"There's a snake in here," she pointed out, because he seemed to be standing there stupidly.

Frantically Aaron remembered why he was here. Yes, there was a snake. Actually, now there were two.

"It won't bite you," he explained in a calm, disembodied voice that had absolutely no connection to the very explicit ideas that were fogging his brain and swelling his cock.

"Do I look like I'm going to put my feet on the floor?"

She wanted him to look? Okay. He looked. Stared. Leered. Discreetly he coughed, clearing the lust from his voice. "What do I need to get out of here? You or the snake? I can heft you out if you'd like."

She shook her head, spraying him with water. Frankly it didn't help. "Heft? Do I look like I need hefting?"

So once again, Aaron obeyed her instructions and looked. Last night he had tried to avoid staring, tried to avoid memorizing every touch, every curve. But in daylight, when the sun shone down on her like a flare, ignorance was impossible.

Against his better judgment he stared, and was ignorant no more. Of course he'd seen women naked before. To be fair, he'd seen more beautiful naked women before, but they didn't affect him quite so viscerally as this one. She was slim and freckled with a silky belly that was finished in a glistening patch of golden-blond—

"The *snake*," she yelled at him. Deservedly.

"Right." Aaron blinked and focused on the snake. It wasn't that big. Not life-threatening. Although it did look slightly aroused.

With a pitying smile, he picked up the little guy and carried him outside where he threw it in the grass. "You've been kicked out, dude. Sorry."

While he watched the snake slide away, he wondered what was he supposed to do now? More torn than he cared to admit, he stared at the open entrance to the showers, trying to decide if he was supposed to go back to the cabin and find the perfect metaphor for the protagonist's final betrayal of everything that he believed in. Or was he supposed to return to the showers?

To check on her. To make sure everything was okay. See if she was calm or needed assistance.

Oh, yeah, Mr. Boy Scout. Who are you fooling with that one?

He walked in, all earnest concern. "Jennifer?" The water was still streaming, and there were no feet on the floor.

"Jennifer?" he asked, feeling something that could be panic lodged in his throat.

Quickly he pulled aside the curtain and took in her pale face. He sighed. No panic necessary. "It's okay now."

"I don't want to touch the floor," she muttered.

"Do you want me to help?" were the first words out of his mouth, which should have been a big clue that something was wrong. Thoughtful? Conscientious? Not in this lifetime.

"Please," she said, and Aaron took a deep breath. He was

going to have to do this. He was going to have to touch her. He would be expected to hold her and there could be no gratuitous touching. This wasn't sexual. This was comfort, and damned if he knew what that entailed. Some men were born with the knack of knowing exactly what to say and what to do. Aaron was not one of them.

"I'm going to step in, and I'll grab you around the waist," he said very precisely, talking to himself, as much as her. "Grab my neck. We'll be fine." He was very proud of that last bit. That was definitely comforting.

He stepped into the stall, water blasting his clothes, and very carefully he locked his hands around her waist. He did not look at the two pert mounds that he had groped under the moon. He did not look at the sun-touched nipples that made his mouth water. Determinedly, he dragged his eyes to her face.

She looked as if she was about to faint.

"Grab my neck," he told her, and felt her arms lock around him in a death grip.

"I hate snakes," she whispered.

"Apparently they like you," he said, carrying her to the bench. He sat down, expecting her to move from his lap, expecting her to leap up and get dressed, but she didn't move.

Oh, God.

Then the tears started.

She had a nice face. A warm gold with splotches of freckles. The water had darkened her hair to the color of wheat at twilight. But it was the eyes that were killing him. Wide, glimmering. Vulnerable.

Aaron hated vulnerable.

He pressed her face against his chest, hiding those soul-destroying eyes before he turned into a man he couldn't respect. "It was a grass snake. No big deal. Couldn't have hurt you if it wanted to."

"It was slimy and it crawled on me," she mumbled, her body shivering from fear, cold and the possible realization that Aaron wasn't good at showing concern.

His hands did not palm her well-formed ass as they yearned to do. Instead they stroked her back. It was awkward and clumsy but she didn't seem to notice. He could smell her shampoo, perfumed and vivid, probably with a name like River Flower or something equally silly. But the artificial smell didn't roll his stomach as it normally would. He liked it.

It was a testament to his steely determination that he could ignore the two unsinkable nipples that were slowly burning a permanent scar into his bare skin until she moved away from him. And yes, finally realizing that modesty did have a prudent purpose in life, she reached for her pile of clothes and held them to her chest.

They almost covered her and a more honorable man might have politely looked away.

"Thank you," she told him, sounding grateful and sincere, as if he had actually helped the situation instead of exploiting it for his own lurid benefit. Her gratitude was a plus.

"Not a big deal," he said casually, all while thinking he'd love to do it again. His body badly wanted sex, but his mind knew better.

Since he'd lived in the cabin, sex hadn't been one of his drives. Nine years ago he'd learned his lesson, learned what happened when the cock ruled the head, but not anymore. Now when he needed sex, he went to another town and found an anonymous naked blonde. For a few hours he would satisfy himself, before returning to his work. There were rules against creating a mess where you slept, so he was careful never to bring sex into the sanctuary he'd made.

Aaron was a cold-blooded SOB that wouldn't think twice about sleeping with Jenn, watching her leave and calmly returning back to his self-styled exile.

Still his gut—the very gut that told him when a scene was off—cramped badly at the thought and told him to leave her alone.

Normally he obeyed his instincts, and Aaron would hack and cut, not worrying about the amount of work that he lost. But not this time.

She would be leaving soon and he might as well take advantage while he could.

While he was still congratulating himself on his new plan, she stood, and again he got that kick in the gut. Okay, Jenn was not shy about her body. What happened to modesty? Modesty was good. Modesty was smart. Modesty kept his cock from forgetting its place.

"I'll get dressed," she said, grabbing a pair of jeans, raising one leg to step into them, her legs splaying in a thoughtless, ordinary manner that caused him to moan.

She stopped, her efficient fingers poised at the base of her fly. "Problem?" she asked, her glistening breasts defying him to utter meaningful words.

Mute, he shook his head. Then, because no, that wasn't enough torture for him, she pulled the thin T-shirt over her wet head, over her still damp flesh, over her perfectly formed breasts.

The useless material dampened to what could only be called transparency, clinging to her curves as faithful and true as his hands longed to do.

"Don't you have a towel?" he croaked.

"Nope," she replied before heading out, leaving Aaron

staring at the space her bare body had occupied only moments before. It was a long time before Aaron could move.

Hell.

4

THE COBBLESTONES THAT rimmed the main square of town would have been hell on tires—if cars were allowed.

The main thoroughfare of Harmony Springs was closed off to all but walking traffic. Possessing a keen marketing skill that Jennifer could admire, the townspeople had long ago suspected that city people would adore walking without horns honking or the fear of being sideswiped from the sidewalk.

The townspeople had been right, Jenn thought. It was a great day for aimlessly walking in the warm sun. Today she'd worn a sleeveless tank, partly playing the role of the wide-eyed tourist, and partly because a little color on her pale arms would be nice. Maybe she wouldn't have a job when she went home, but she'd have a tan. It wasn't going to put food on the table, but she clung to the thought.

Actually, while she strolled through the town, it wasn't too hard to be a tourist. The store windows were strategically designed to attract the eye with richly colored glass of blues and reds and greens. Old-fashioned toys spilled out of paisley-lined trunks.

Diamonds and gold gleamed in the window of the local jeweler. And then there were the clothes. A woman could spend a fortune in this town on clothes. And most required washing by hand.

What a crock, what a scam…what a great little skirt in royal-blue, and it would be perfect against the new tan that she was developing. She was just contemplating the overpriced tag, wondering if food was really a necessary requirement for survival, when her phone rang.

Oh, yes, yes! Oh, brave new world that hadn't forgotten her.

On the other end was Martina DiCarlo, a coworker at the paper, sometime drinking buddy, longtime friend in times of misery and need.

"You've got a problem," Martina stated, a happy way to kick off a conversation.

"Worse than my existing problem?"

"A gazillion times worse. Quinn's given Lizette the Palermo scandal."

Martina was right. It was worse. "My story on the Harmony Springs Summer Nights Festival will be measured against the shocking downfall of one of the most beloved members of the city council?"

"Looks that way."

"Tell me why I wanted to do this job?"

"You wanted to right the wrongs in the world. You wanted to fight for truth, justice, and the American Way."

Yes, Martina was making a joke, but there was a certain truth in it. "God, I was a sap."

"When you said it, I thought it sounded noble. Sappy, naive but noble."

"What am I going to do?"

"Enjoy the vacation, plot new career strategies. *That,* my friend, is the American Way."

"I'm getting a tan. Freckles." Objectively she studied

her arms. "Okay, it's a slight sunburn. You know, I would enjoy the vacation part if my cabin was a little nicer. We have community showers," she started, then trailed off as she remembered the events of this morning, the sight of her hero fumbling his way into a rescue, the dazed shock in his eyes as she shamelessly flaunted her nakedness in front of him.

Those were good times.

Little did she suspect that one-star accommodations could actually be fun.

Suddenly a sneaking suspicion occurred to her, probably only because of its very deviousness. "Did Lizette have anything to do with my travel reservations?"

Martina hummed for a bit, the way she did when she was thinking. "Well, Alfonse handles the bookings. He likes short skirts and see-through blouses, and I'd lay odds his professional ethics could be bent."

Yes, another woman using her seductive wiles to get what she wanted. That hussy. "She did it. I know it. Lizette sidled in there, asking for a little favor, all while leaning over his desk, fluttering those come-hither lashes like he was the sexiest man alive. Poor Alfonse never stood a chance."

"Want me to confirm?" asked Martina, ever the intrepid reporter.

However, Jenn knew a good opportunity for self-pity when she heard it. Right now, in absence of chocolate-fudge-brownie ice cream, she needed it. "No need for verification. Even if she didn't, I'd feel better thinking she did, so let me savor my petty grievances."

"She *is* sleeping with Howard. That's not so petty."

"You're right. That's downright shitty. See? You cheered me up. Be proud, Martina. You've done your good deed for the day."

"So, any great leads up there? Something exciting?"

"The exciting kind of something that will move papers?"

"Does that question to a question indicate there is something exciting?"

"No, there's nothing," answered Jenn, not wanting to sound defensive but sounding defensive.

Martina, being a good and true friend, knew denial when she heard it, laughed in that mocking scoffing you-can't-lie-to-a-good-and-true-friend sort of way. "There are only three things that can make a woman sound like that—going overbudget on clothes, gorging on food or going down on a man."

"My emotional happiness is not dependent on the influence of a man."

"Is your name Gloria Steinem? Do you own a vibrator? If the answer to these questions are no and no, then yes, your sexual happiness is dependent on a man."

"I own a vibrator. And you said sexual happiness," she argued. "I said emotional."

"Which is an excellent point, diverting the conversation from the more important questions, who is he, how did you meet him and is he providing you with sexual happiness?"

"You're such a slut," shot back Jenn, a diversionary tactic designed to hide her recent foray into diversions.

"Please, you are so transparent. Gratuitous name-calling will not sway me from my purpose, and only make me more curious about what you're hiding."

"I'm not hiding anything," protested Jenn.

"Has he seen you naked?"

"Does everybody have to keep talking about naked?"

"Aha! He has seen you naked! Now who's the slut, slut?"

"We haven't had sex."

"Full-frontal foreplay without stealing home? Fascinating. It gives him depth, character, mystery. Where does he live? Lower East Side? Tribeca?"

"Harmony Springs."

"Oh, honey. I'm sorry. Does he have all his teeth?"

Jenn snorted in disgust. Why, it sounded exactly like her two days ago. "Do you know how shallow and prejudicial that sounds? There are many people in this town who have excellent dental health. More so than the city frankly."

"So why does he live there? Why doesn't he live in Manhattan?"

"I don't know." It was the mystery to end all mysteries. He didn't have the small town vibe about him, that easygoing friendliness that populated small towns all over America.

"Maybe he likes the small town life better?"

Jenn considered it for a minute. "Is that possible?"

"I don't think so." Martina was silent, mulling the idea. "What the hell. Ask him. Unless you, Ms. 'I Live To Poke In People's Lives,' have suddenly gotten shy."

No, shyness had never been her problem. "I asked. He avoided."

"Do you need help? I could take the train up there," Martina volunteered, because in many ways she was just as nosy as Jenn. "We could do good cop, bad cop. I'll be good cop, you can be bad cop. You're a lot meaner than I am."

"Don't come up here."

"Why?"

"I have work to do. Real work. This isn't a vacation. This is my life. What am I going to do if I get laid off?"

"It's going to be okay. Labor numbers are looking good."

"What about the April circulation numbers for the paper?"

"Eh…. They could be better."

"Thank you for being honest. Depressing but honest."

"You're going to be fine, Jenn. You're good at what you do. Worst case, if Lizette ends up staying and you're cut, you'll land somewhere else."

Martina made it sound too easy, but Jenn had clawed and schlepped her way up the ladder, and her nature did not lend itself to clawing and schlepping. She was better at shooting the breeze and chewing the fat.

"Do you know the lectures I'm going to get from my parents? The unsaid I-told-you-so's which are so much worse than the real I-told-you-so's because you both know they're thinking it, so why not say it? Since I was eight, I've had to listen to 'pick a viable career.' And what's journalism? Chopped liver? I tell you, it's enough to make me whine and kvetch incessantly, repetitively and every other -ly adverb that I'm supposed to avoid."

"You do get redundant when it comes to your parents, repeating the same thing over and over, ad nauseum et cetera."

Jenn started to laugh, glad that Martina had called. Friends were good. Friends were comfortable. Friends reminded her not to second-guess herself. As opposed to family, who made her question herself on a regular basis.

"Sorry for the replay. I suppose I'm wasting your minutes. I'll shut up now and go seek out cool and interesting things to write about."

"You sound stressed. You know what works for stress? Sex."

"Hanging up now," Jenn said, and pressed the disconnect button.

Immediately her phone beeped again. No call, just a text message. Get laid.

Jenn popped her phone into her purse and sighed.

Orgasms should have counted as stress-busters, but somehow the anticipation of more only made the stress worse.

LATE THAT AFTERNOON SHE discovered Frank's Ice Cream and Carbs. At first she thought it was a slap in the face to dieters everywhere, but once inside she discovered that the carb in the name referred to carburetors, not carbohydrates.

Clever.

Already she liked Frank, whoever he was.

She was.

Frank was actually Frankie, a crusty old redhead with grease on her coveralls and a pink bandana in her hair. Instantly Jenn was curious. The store was a small ice-cream parlor with a working garage next door. Apparently Frankie was not only chief mechanic, but also head ice-cream scooper, as well. Dual-career opportunities. Smart, very smart.

Frankie was buried under the open hood of a car, and Jenn ducked her head low in order to see…a lot of dirt and grease and car stuff. "So how did you end up as a mechanic?" she asked.

The woman poked at the engine, and then wiped at her face, leaving two streaks of grease. Jenn realized that if she took up auto repair, her parents would have a heart attack. "Got started by necessity more than anything. Had a 1976 Opal. Piece of shit car that always broke down. I was working four jobs to keep the car running, but eventually I told myself, 'Self, you need to rise above this one. You need to learn to fix cars.' Now, in Peekskill where I lived, there was quite a few mechanics, but in Harmony Springs? Nada. After very little debate, I decided to buy out the ice-cream parlor, build out a few bays and ta-da. Originally it was Frankie's, but the town patriarchy was nervous about entrusting their precious wheels to a woman. Sexist pigs. So I changed the name to Frank's, and eventually my multitude of skills won them over."

She rubbed her hands on the blue coveralls, looking comfortably knee-deep in grease. Another contented resident. A cheery bell dinged, signaling a customer in the store. Jenn followed after her, watching as Frankie washed her hands, put on a red-striped apron and then dipped two scoops of Rocky Road for a freckle-faced kid. Inside the store were a small group of metal parlor tables, and two old men playing chess, and in the far corner, someone was hidden behind a copy of the *Times*.

"How long have you lived here?"

"Long enough. Too long."

"You know anything about an old literary group that used to meet up here? Some famous book types is what I heard. Is that true or just marketing spin?"

In the corner, the newspaper shook, and Jenn looked over, wondering exactly who was behind the newspaper and then told herself to get back on task.

"Book people?" Frankie laughed, not an encouraging sound. "Don't know that. I usually didn't ask who did what or how the engine gaskets get blown. You got some names?"

"No. Just some old articles that made it sound like some hush-hush weekend gatherings."

Frankie brushed a strand of hair from her face and then thought for a minute. "There was a group of psychics. A metaphysical guru, but they didn't believe in cars. If you ask Sheriff Phelps, he might help you out."

"Psychics? Real ones?"

"Is there such a thing?" she asked, one hand cocked on her hip.

"I guess not," answered Jenn, not that she wanted to believe in psychics, but the plausibility of a paranormal reality made for great reading. She leaned over the glass ice-cream case, eyeing the flavors, and realized that it was almost time for lunch.

"You have chocolate-fudge-brownie ice cream here?"

"I have chocolate fudge. I have brownies. Want me to smash them up for you?"

"Yeah."

"And if you write this one up, make you sure you get the name right." Frankie dipped the scoop in hot water and prepared to make some high-fat paranormal magic. It wouldn't make news, but it made happiness. Jenn would take what she could get.

DIDI SHOWED UP precisely at noon, which was proof of her more bloodthirsty nature, but today Aaron was prepared. Today he'd fought a harmless snake and won. Today he'd braved a naked Jennifer, and nearly survived the experience.

After all that, Didi seemed almost mundane. But to be on the safe side, he'd scattered papers here and there, marked up pages and opened the Oxford English Dictionary to the letter *M*. In short, he looked like a writer buried in his work.

"You have been busy, I see," she pronounced, picking up a discarded page, before he grabbed it out of her hands. "How can you abide this prison? There are no skyscrapers, no pastrami, and…you've forgotten to shave. Are you chopping wood and wearing flannel, as well? Oy." She dusted the seat of his battered rocker, but eventually gave up and stood, casting him a damning look in the process because being uncooperative was what Didi did best. They had that in common.

"Did you bring the food?" he asked.

"Squash, ground lamb and the bone meal. A diet without calcium is not good for your bones. You should take supplements, too. I brought you a bottle, but I'm sure you'll only throw them away."

The cat jumped at the food and sniffed, yowling with hunger, and Didi shooed him away.

"You shouldn't push him away. The food isn't for me. It's his."

Her eyes widened in alarm. "I carried takeout for your cat?"

"Do you know what they put in cat food?"

She lifted her hands, warding off the thought. "I do not choose to know. Instead of working, you stagnate here playing Top Chef for this ragged monster?"

At that, Two crouched low to the ground and showed leonine teeth.

"He has to eat," Aaron defended.

"As do I." Uncaring of the dust, she collapsed in the rocker, her hand over her chest. "I cannot do this any longer."

Immediately Aaron backtracked, feeling something cold and clammy close up in his throat. "You can't leave me."

"I'm an old woman, Aaron."

"You've got a good thirty years of spite left in you."

She wasn't amused. "And you? What is left in you? Did he steal it all?"

Quickly he rose and pulled the food from the box, Two perched protectively on the cabinets, overseeing the process. He chose not to answer Didi, because he didn't know what was inside him. Whatever remained, he used for his writing, and nothing else. It worked.

Two batted a paw at the lamb, awaiting supper. Unlike Didi, Aaron recognized that this wasn't companionship but survival. The cat wore his scars on the outside, but Aaron didn't have any scars. A long time ago, he'd been drained of blood and life. All that he'd kept safe was his imagination, and Cecil Barksdale would never get at that.

"You owe me a book, a chapter, even a sentence. Or I will leave you. Like that," Didi threatened with a snap of her fingers.

"Do what you need to do," he said with a careless shrug, seeing the pain in her eyes, but he wouldn't be cornered, not even by Didi.

She rose just as carelessly, just as heartlessly. Their relationship was back to what it should be, exactly as he needed. Aaron began to breathe once again.

"You'll be back?" he asked, carefully erasing all trace of expectation from his voice.

Didi being Didi wasn't fooled, but her smile was old and weary and he wondered how long it would be before she left him for good.

"Thank you for the food," he told her politely.

She adjusted her shawl, flinging it over her shoulder, and then made for the door, her heels never missing a beat. "When will you learn, Aaron? When will you rejoin the human race?"

"Never," he said, his voice firm and stubborn, but Didi had already left, and he told himself that he didn't care.

5

IN THE 1960s, A MERRY band of psychics had occupied the rolling hills to the north, and when psychics were involved, law enforcement wouldn't be far behind, and Jenn knew just where to find the truth.

In Harmony Springs, Sheriff Omar Phelps was the long arm of the law, and unsurprisingly enough, his arms were very long. He wore the usual khaki uniform and badge, but on top of his head was a beaten-up Yankees cap.

His office was in the basement of the courthouse and consisted of a wooden desk and chair, a shelf full of baseball trophies and what she assumed to be the Phelps family photo. All in all, the office seemed quiet and serene, no crime, no small-town hijinx, and Jenn tried not to look disappointed.

"Tell me about the psychic community. Were you sheriff then?" she asked, once the introductions were done.

"I was a deputy, and didn't know shit from shinola, but I've learned. Grifters, that was my guess, but they attracted a long following of gullible marks." He leaned back in his wooden chair, and kicked his boots up on the desk.

"Any colorful anecdotes, famous names that might have been conned?" Jenn asked, because debunked tales of the paranormal always attracted attention, even better if the rich and famous were involved. If there was a politician, a Rockefeller, a Carnegie, or a Roosevelt, heck, her career woes could be over.

He laughed at her, but his eyes were nice, in that I-bet-you-believe-in-Santa-Claus sort of way. "We didn't get a lot of real names from the marks. Back then, people didn't brag about getting conned. Not like today." He gave her a nod, one professional to the other. "But you know that."

"What about the literary salons? The group of writers who came up. Any truth to that one?" Jenn braced a hip against the desk, making notes as they talked.

"Maybe," he answered with a shrug to his beefy shoulders.

"What do you mean?"

"Before I took over, I heard some stories, looked up some reports."

"And?"

"A lot of drunk and disorderlies, one goat smuggled into the steeple of the church, four cases of vandalism and one desecration of a grave. Nothing serious, but a lot of payoffs."

"Who was involved?" she asked casually, thinking a governor would be nice. Or a governor's family.

"Juliet Capulet and Madonna Ciccone and Mamie Eisenhower."

"The first lady?" she asked, excitement coloring her normally professional tone, because first ladies trumped governors every time.

The man laughed at her, slapping his knee, because apparently this was jaw-dropping fun. "Nah. They were fake names."

Glad somebody had a sense of humor. "Doesn't anybody show proper ID in this town?" she mused.

"Not much. The law can be bought," he answered, scratching his ear. "Or at least, back then it could. But I want to state for the record that I don't take bribes and never have."

She studied the man with careful eyes. No. He knew his job, he did his job, and then went on his way. It seemed like everybody in this town knew their place and worked their tail off to stay there. It was a good way to be. She could be that. All she had to do was keep digging.

Hope sprang eternal inside her, or perhaps that was hunger. No. Definitely hope and optimism. Undaunted, Jenn handed the man her number. "If you remember anything, give me a call, will you?"

"Will do."

After two more trips to the library and the archives of the *Harmony Herald,* she was ready to pursue the promise of food, preferably something high in calories and fat, accompanied by a triple shot of espresso. Healthy? No. Spirit-lifting? Hell, yes.

It was at that moment that her mother called, possessing a maternal ESP that immediately senses the ever-elastic soul in peril.

Certainly when Jenn had been a kid, it had been fun having the loving mother who was always a little older than the other mothers. Jenn's mother had been the one who made sure she had extra raisins in her lunch, the one that read stories to her every night, and then explained how the intestine clogged up every time it had to process unsaturated fats.

Now that Jenn was out on her own, sometimes her mother forgot.

"Hello, Mom," she answered, standing outside the Hungry Hobo, trying to decide between a double cheeseburger with avocado and fries or skipping straight to dessert—a chocolate-mocha cheesecake coated in a white chocolate ganache. The cheesecake was winning.

"How are you doing, sweetie?"

"I'm doing fine."

"You haven't been laid off yet, have you? You'd tell me, wouldn't you?"

The thought of layoffs cemented the decision. Definitely the cheesecake. Life was too short to forget dessert. "I'm not laid off yet, but the day's still young."

"I read about the cutbacks at the *Times*. I worried. Did you see that article?"

"Yes, that is my paper. I do read it. Daily."

"I didn't think they'd have it up there."

"Floored me, too. And indoor plumbing, can you believe it?" *Just not in my cabin.* "It's not the boondocks, Mom. Besides, I get the news on my phone. It's really cool."

"You shouldn't have bought the phone, Jennifer. You can't afford it."

"Yeah, but since I'm about to lose my job anyway, what's a little more red ink?"

"You could come and work at the hospital with me. We need someone in payroll. It's not as glamorous as journalism, but the salary is better. And the benefits are good, too."

"I don't want to work at the hospital. My stomach doesn't have the Kevlar coating that yours does. I'm a journalist."

"I know that's what you think you want to do, but how do you know, Jennifer? When you were seven, you wanted to be an astronaut."

"And now I'm twenty-seven."

"When I was twenty-seven, your father and I had bought our first apartment."

"Real estate was very cheap back then. I rent."

"But it's not very smart, Jennifer. How can you be comfortable with that decision?"

"I feel very comfortable with that decision."

"I'm sorry. I'm pushing, aren't I? Henry said that I'm pushing you too hard, and I should back off. But these are hard times, and I love you, and I worry about you."

"I know, Mom. I'm going to be fine."

"If you need anything…"

"I'll let you know if I end up starving or without heat—"

"Did they shut off your power? Oh, Jenn!"

"I was joking, Mom."

"Well, you know your roommate is going to move on without you one of these days, and then where will you be?"

"Without a roommate," she tried, not that her mother would see the humor.

"Wouldn't you rather have a cat?"

"A cat won't pay rent, Mom. People can be useful that way."

"How's your room up there? Are you locking your doors? There's a lot of strangers up there, and you don't know who you'll meet—"

"I'm in a great place," she interrupted, thinking fast. "It's this huge Victorian with clawfoot tubs and they have a security guard in the lobby, in this bright scarlet blazer with gold tassels. You'd really like him. His name is Oliver, and he's British."

"Really?" Out of everything, it was the British that tickled her mother. "Oh, good. I was nervous about you being there alone."

Sometimes she made up stories to give her mother hope, and it made her mother happy. Perhaps Dr. Dade suspected the truth, but Jenn didn't think so. Those romantic, idealistic genes singing happily inside Jenn came from somewhere. Ironic that the very traits that she'd passed onto her daughter were the ones that worried Jenn's mother the most. Or maybe that was the point of family. You got who you got, no matter who you hoped they'd turn into. And when you finally accepted them, then you knew there was love.

"I love you, Mom, but listen, I have to go."

After that conversation, Jenn looked over the menu, felt the slow hardening of her arteries, and with a dejected sigh, she walked away.

Twenty-seven years old, and the power of the parental suggestion still worked over distance, cell connections and sometimes without talking at all.

Darn it.

JENN HAD MADE PEACE with her decision to forgo the cheesecake. She'd spent the afternoon at the computer with a carrot stick in her mouth, but when her phone struck eleven, she wasn't so disciplined as to ignore the lure of the rock.

The moon was a slim sliver, the stars obscured by clouds, and still she sat there like the world's most dedicated Galileo, watching for a man who stirred her senses instead of watching for the stars. In her heart of hearts, she knew that even Galileo took a night off every now and again.

It was nearly eleven-thirty when he showed, and right on target, her pulse leaped.

"How was the day today?" he asked, amazingly polite and cordial, not even bothering to complain about her phone.

She leaned back on her palms, gazing up at the stars. Dedicated, diligent, not wanting to get laid. Hopefully he was fooled. "I discovered that the Psychic Hotline originated up here. And there was a lot of hard-partying bookish types, all very cute human interest, but I was hoping to find something a little meatier."

"You could write about your adventures with snakes."

"Very funny."

"It's only day two. How long are you going to stay?"

"Two weeks. Maybe less."

"You'll find something," he assured her.

"Why are you being nice tonight?" she asked because it was possible that he had evolved into Everyman, saying what he thought women wanted to hear to get laid.

"The writing went well," he stated cheerfully.

"Did you kill me off today?" she asked, secretly hoping that he did. She liked that she was the bane of his existence.

"I did," he answered, thrilling her more than he would ever know. "You were left alone in the desert, and the vultures came and pecked at your nude body until only a skeleton remained."

"Fixated on that nude thing, aren't you?" she taunted, homing in on the important parts.

He shrugged, but she wasn't fooled. For a few minutes they sat, and she very deliberately played with her phone, waiting for a snide remark or some indication of sexual awareness, but he seemed off someplace else—someplace not on her rock.

When the silence stretched on, she realized that she didn't have the patience to out-wait him.

"Why did you leave last night?" she asked because it was a conundrum and she wanted to understand.

"Fixated on that analysis thing, aren't you?"

"Curious. I noticed the large evidence of frustration on your part."

"You don't take rejection well, do you?" he retorted

with a hint of frustration. She deemed it sexual instead of personal.

"About as well as you handle sexual frustration. I think we're both hiding deep neuroses, probably due to some long-erased memory of trauma at an early age."

"Speak for yourself. I'm normal," he stated, sounding as if he believed it.

She chose not to correct him because he would argue and protest and she'd had too long of a day for that. Really, all she wanted was to sit in the company of someone who was more unsettled than her. It made her feel...content.

"What's the problem with your parents?" he asked, breaking the silence, but he seemed genuinely interested, and she liked that he wanted to know more about her. So she told him the truth. The real truth. The one that kept her in cheesecakes and chocolate.

"I don't want to listen to my parents. I don't want to think they're right. But what if they're right? What if this is a pipe dream? I've been busting my butt for five years, and it's hard. What if I'm not cut out for hard? What if I'm one of those mealymouthed people who always take the easy way out, never actually achieving anything because it's too difficult, and I don't think I can do it?"

There. She'd said it, and the world did not explode. The omnipotent ghost of mothers everywhere did not pop out and scream, "Aha! I knew it."

"You shouldn't undermine yourself. People will do whatever it takes if they truly want something. Including you." It sounded incredibly pithy and encouraging. The words she'd hear from a well-meaning friend, not a man committed to absolute truth.

"Ah, yes, words of wisdom from a man who lives his life from an isolated cabin in the woods."

"You're mocking me," he said, which, she noticed, wasn't

a denial. It was comforting to sit in the company of someone who understood her issues. The doubt that occurred when you flew in the face of conventional wisdom.

She gave him a foolish smile. "You mocked yourself first. I thought that gave me permission to reciprocate in kind."

"Cheeky."

"I prefer the words *fearless* and *directed*."

"And you said that exactly like any fearless and self-directed person would," he encouraged, daring to touch her hand. It was only a quick skim of her knuckles, but her nerves jumped just the same. She knew what it cost him, that momentary breakdown of his defenses.

Feeling happier, she pointed up at the sky, the very sky that had watched her writhe and moan last night. She liked sitting in the cloak of night, similar to the cloak of anonymity in the city, but here there was a jump in her senses, or maybe that was Aaron.

"Do you know the name of that group of stars up there?"

"Are you really asking me if I want to learn about the world from a phone?" he answered in a tone that indicated pigs would be more likely to fly.

"I won't ask," she stated fearlessly. "You strike me as a man who is on a humbling journey to a more enlightened place of being. I'm just going to assume."

He nodded to her phone. "Why do you like that so much?"

"It's a GPS, a coffee-finder, a time-management tool and a calorie counter. All the things that I lack."

"You're lazy," he pronounced, but his tone was indulgent and warm, coming from a man who was accepting of his own flawed nature.

"I prefer the term self-aware," she defended. "And I don't

think that it's laziness. More a pattern of distraction in my life."

"I'm one of your distractions, aren't I?"

"Definitely," she told him, happy to assign the blame where it belonged. And woohoo, it wasn't her. "What about your parents?"

She had decided that he was a trust-fund baby. Neglected yet spoiled, shunning the trappings of a material world.

"Mom died young. My father raised me."

And Jenn would bet her eyeteeth that it was his nanny that raised him, or some caring teacher at boarding school. "How did she die? Cancer? That's got to be hard on a kid."

"Suicide."

He said it so evenly, like it was a sale at Saks or a long wait for a cab. Nothing out of the ordinary at all. She watched him from under her lashes, but there were absolutely zero indications that he hurt at all.

"I'm sorry."

"She was depressed. My father was probably the root of her depression. I don't know. Anyway, I was too little to suffer from it."

This time she caught it. That cheerful invincibility in his voice, as if nothing phased him at all. Ah, yes, denial. She knew that one well. "I'm sorry," she said, and meant it. Her parents had always been a constant in her life, perhaps not the most comfortable constant, but she never doubted them, and she hurt for anyone who didn't have that security. And she hurt even more for the man who pretended *he* didn't need it.

He met her eyes, cool and composed. "I'm not the only kid to grow up without a mother."

"What was your father like?"

"Tell me about the constellations," he asked, not so neatly changing the subject.

"And now you want to know?"

"It's either that or fool around," he muttered, finally sounding like a man who wanted to get laid. Jenn couldn't quite hide her smile. Later they would talk. Right now he needed to be held, to be comforted, to be loved. And of course, she'd never say that.

"I'd prefer not to have sex on a rock," she said instead.

"Very provincial."

"My bed's like a rock." It was a strong hint to see his cabin. To pry deeper into his life.

"Then why not take your pleasure under the stars?" he asked, remaining maddeningly clueless. "It's a nice night. In the summer, you have to take advantages of the opportunities as they're presented."

"Come on," she said, taking his hand, and leading him back to her place, the land of the bedrock mattress. With his sensibilities, he probably wouldn't notice. Martina would call her a masochist, headed for a heartbreak, and her mother would only shake her head with a sigh, but right now Jenn needed Aaron. And right now—no matter what he believed—Aaron needed Jenn. Sometimes that was the most important thing in the world.

6

HER CABIN WAS APPALLING. The bed was worse than the rock. There was a cricket in the corner, and he swore there was something jabbing into his spine.

Aaron was in heaven.

He kept his watch on his wrist, determined to keep track of the time, determined to prove that he was in complete control.

Of course, that was before she took off her shirt.

In the meager light, he thought her smile might have been a bit smug, but the windows were caked with dust, and the moonlight was dim, so he might have been mistaken, or at least he hoped he was.

He waited precisely three seconds before he touched her, and by the time he'd finished counting, his hands were shaking and his cock was about to explode, and he told himself that it would better not to wait next time.

Assuming that there was a next time, he reminded himself.

Then his mouth was locked to her breast, and her fingers were pressing into his hair, and it was very difficult to think.

She jerked at the hem of his shirt, pulling it over his

head, and then she fell on him, or perhaps, more truthfully, he fell on her, and they were tumbling to the bed where he felt the painful crack of his head. He yelled out loud, and she kissed his head, his neck, his mouth, and the pain diminished into a different sort of pain.

A decadent pain.

He tugged at her jeans, getting her naked, and in the absence of light, he used his hands, his mouth to undress her. Judging by the staccato gasps, she didn't seem to mind. When he laved at her breast, he could feel her nipples swell in his mouth. It was such a heady sensation. Better than Scotch, better than the numb burn of whiskey. This was life. In the dark, there was nothing but this. But her. His hands stroked between her legs, and she was damp and aroused and waiting for him there.

It was a testament to his steadfastness that he didn't just ram into her right then. No. He wanted her to explode. He wanted her to want. He wanted her to scream. For him.

Selfishly, because he wanted more, he used his mouth on her, his tongue at her naval, following the path of her skin. He could taste the salt and the sun, and the light inside her that the night couldn't dim. When he kissed her there, when he thrust his tongue inside her, she gasped, her hips rising, and he smiled with satisfaction.

Yes. He'd done that, he thought.

Every time that he tasted her, every time he sucked on her flesh, she would cry out, her fingernails raking against his back, and he'd never heard any sound that was so sweet, so erotic, so cock-torturous.

But Aaron was strong, working to kick his body in check. This was about proving that he didn't need her, didn't need this, so he licked harder against her skin, feeling the moisture on his tongue, feeling her spasms, and knowing that he was driving her mad.

Just as she'd done to him.

It only seemed fair.

Her hands fisted in his hair, pulling and pressing, and she began to mutter and swear, and he nearly laughed at that.

Madness was the very best sort of lust. The loss of the barriers, the complete dissolution of a person, all the pretense taken away, and only a mass of vulnerabilities remained.

And she was there.

Harder he worked her, hearing the deep shallows of her breath, knowing she was nearly there. Wanting her there, he plunged his finger inside her, and her body rose, possessed by a demon, possessed by him, and she froze for a moment, until finally, with a quiet scream, she fell.

This time, the role of the Boy Scout came easier, and Aaron gathered her close in his arms and stroked her hair, his hand guarding the beat of her heart. He listened for the languor in her breathing, the small signs of sleep. There was no light in the cabin, nothing to keep the darkness at bay—except for her.

After she had slipped into her dreams, very carefully he detached himself from her and put on his shirt. For a long second he stayed, peering into the blackness, and knowing she was there. But in the end, he walked out her door, and walked through the woods, back to his cabin.

It wasn't difficult to leave her. In fact, he told himself, he didn't even regret the raging throb in his pants. He was no slave to emotion or pleasure. He was only a slave to his art.

The cat eyed him cautiously, but Aaron wasn't planning to sleep or ease the pain in his cock. Instead he lit the candle on top of his desk, then sat in front of his typewriter and let the pain flow into his words.

JENN AWOKE ALONE, and she wondered if she'd dreamed the whole thing, but her jeans were on the floor, her shirt was tossed over a chair and there was a mark on her breast. His mark. Not that she cared. Really.

Quickly she threw on fresh clothes, and looked over her scrambled notes from yesterday. Yeah, she needed coffee, yeah, she needed to wake up her brain, but first she needed to do this. To sit down and work. To focus. To prove to herself that she could.

It wasn't a great start. The beginning wasn't nearly as clever as she wanted it to be, and she blamed it on the fog in her head, and not the wicked throb between her thighs.

Sure, she'd gotten off last night, but she'd been the only one, and she wondered why he didn't trip the light fantastic, as well. Was there a problem? With him? With her?

Instead of looking at her screen, she stared at the demolition site that had been her bed, and sighed.

Not smart, Jenn. Not smart at all.

Clearing the fog from her mind, she pulled on her sneakers, sprayed bug repellent and sunblock on her arms, and decided to scavenge her morning cup of coffee.

When she opened the door, she almost missed the paper bag, but then she tripped over it, making missing it pretty much impossible.

Inside were two yellow bath towels, plump and soft to the touch. Jenn had almost convinced herself that Carolyn had put them on her doorstep, struck by a neighborly bout of sympathy. Happy with the idea of having something luxurious, she buried her nose in the downy fabric, and inhaled.

Not Carolyn.

She knew that scent. She knew that smell. Not a spring-fresh fabric softener, but a musky smell that made her thighs start to tingle all over again.

Aaron?

Seriously?

From the distance she heard the bedlam of his type-writer, and she knew better than to disturb the man who was perpetually disturbed. So she put the towels back in her cabin, and then went off in search of her coffee.

However, as she passed by his cabin she smiled, because in her heart she knew he was killing her all over again.

THE MANHATTAN NEWSPAPERS were always delivered at 6:00 a.m., seven days a week, holidays included.

Aaron had a passionate love-hate relationship with the papers, especially on Thursday.

On Thursday the book section came out and books were both celebrated and pilloried with the stroke of a pen.

His first impulse was to be at Frank's place at the crack of dawn, waiting for the truck. But people would take that to mean that he cared. So Aaron waited until precisely 3:00 p.m., at which time he moseyed down to Frank's, whistling aimlessly, usually pausing to admire some arbitrary piece of rock.

Today, he left at 3:20 p.m., rather than at three, because in his manuscript he had subjected the golden-haired female to a tender love scene and he liked it, which he knew boded ill. Eventually he threw out the scene, changed it to a tragic death off a cliff, and if Two watched him with a particularly knowing look, then Aaron ignored the cat.

There were very few creatures that ranked below Aaron in emotional intelligence, but a half-blind feline was one.

When he strolled through the glass doors at Frank's, no one seemed to notice that he was late. Jacob and Isaiah were hovered over the chessboard, and Isaiah was retelling the story of how he once beat at famous baseball player at chess.

"It's not a lot of work to beat a baseball player at chess," Aaron pointed out, grabbing his paper and settling into the corner where he wouldn't be disturbed.

"You ever beat a baseball player at chess?" asked Jacob, seeing the remark for what it was—Aaron's version of hello, and returning it in kind.

Aaron chose not to respond.

"Didn't think so," Isaiah said to whomever was listening.

Aaron only rattled his paper in response. When Jennifer entered the store, he was halfway through the City Section and it annoyed him the way that the two old men fawned over her as if they'd never been around an attractive female before, but since they were each over sixty, he sat silently in his corner, and didn't mind it too much.

Until Stewart Connelly came in. Yes, Stewart was nice, fortysomething, once divorced with bright red hair that made him look like a kid. And yes, he was the elementary school principal, but did he have to fall all over her, his tongue lapping the ground?

Silently Aaron started to seethe, trying to concentrate on the nominees for the Booker Prize while he listened to the smarm in Stewart's voice, which a gullible female might mistake for boyish sincerity.

"Are you going to the dance?" asked the Boy Wonder.

Of course she was, you pea-brained idiot. It's why she was here.

"Definitely," she told him, more polite than she should have been. Or perhaps she saved all her snarky insults for Aaron, which made him smile behind the safe cover of newsprint.

"You'll save me a dance?" Stewart asked, and Aaron reminded himself that it was a free country, and Jennifer would be smart to get to know Stewart and pump him for information.

Jennifer left a few seconds later, and Aaron breathed a sigh of relief, until Stewart left and Jacob and Isaiah started the colorful rehash, as if everyone in the room hadn't heard each sentimental detail.

"I think Stewart has a thing for her," said Isaiah in that folksy old-timer voice of someone who remembers love as tender and gentle instead of the bitch-slap it actually was.

"In all my days I don't think I've ever seen a man lusting so badly. Like watching a tiny acorn grow into some giant gnarled oak. You just can't predict how tall and twisted it's going to end up." Jacob laughed as if it was somehow funny.

Aaron blocked out the agonies of the conversation and refocused on baseball, wondering why people bothered with the Mets anymore.

"She's too sophisticated for Stewart," Isaiah commented.

"She's too smart," Aaron muttered under his breath, wondering why everyone didn't know that instinctively—like Aaron did.

Jacob smacked at Aaron's newspaper, narrowly missing his nose. "What? You said something, Aaron?"

"Nothing," he answered, detaching himself from the conversation, determined not to listen, because he didn't care.

Jacob moved his king, giving Isaiah a merciful way to end the misery cleverly disguised as a game. Isaiah always won, but some days, the game was longer than others. "Bet he wants to take her home," he said, taking a sip of his tea.

"Maybe he'll get her drunk?" suggested Isaiah, moving his knight, calling out Check.

"He's an elementary school principal. He couldn't get Keith Richards drunk."

Aaron wasn't so sure. Stewart had a long track record with the ladies, usually buying them flowers and books of poetry. The bastard was slime.

"You think she'll let him kiss her?"

"I'm thinking so."

Aaron studied the forecast, and noted the heavy humidity in the area, which explained the sweat at his brow.

"Maybe I'll go to the dance," Isaiah said, and Aaron frowned because a dance was a ridiculous thing, frequented by frivolous people who believed that shoes were meant to be worn out.

"You still got a suit that fits you? You've gotten a little padded in your old age."

"I do indeed. Do you think the widow Newberry will save me a dance?"

"One dollar says not in this lifetime."

Isaiah shook his hand and smiled. "You have a bet."

THAT FRIDAY, THE WEATHER was warm and sultry on the opening night of the festival. A weekend of music, mouth-watering food, mood-altering wine, bargain-hunting and crowds that were as large as those at Christmas. They were predicting rain later that night, and the air was thick with it. But for now, the humidity hung low, shimmering below the clouds.

The dance was held in an old half-ruined icehouse that was open to the elements. Ivy-covered brick columns rose on all sides, and grass peeked through the brick floor. There were no ceilings, no walls, nothing but the columns that stood like soldiers. The music was an eclectic mix that held no discernable pattern. One minute rock, the next Patsy Cline, but all were dance tunes. Tripping the light fantastic was the purpose, and the people of New York had descended in droves.

Jenn found a cedar picnic table near the edge and watched the dancers move around the floor. There were older couples that did the polka in spite of their age, young couples that swayed to some private beat, and huge packs of teenagers that did nothing but jump up and down.

"Do you mind? I won't interrupt your work."

It was Stewart Connelly and although she'd known he would be there, she was still disappointed that it wasn't Aaron. She wanted to see him tonight. She wanted to dance with him. She wanted to lie naked underneath him with nothing but the stars overhead.

Politely she quashed her disappointment and focused on her work. "Tell me about the dance," she suggested, motioning for him to take a seat. "Are those all out-of-towners?"

"Some. The locals complain about parking and crowds, and I guarantee there's somebody getting towed at the high school for illegal parking."

"Strict cops?" she asked, noting how nice he looked, how respectful and stable. Stewart Connelly was the very model of the Modern Major General. Her mother would have approved.

"The tickets are for revenue generation," he said.

She leaned in farther and plastered a fascinated look on her face. "How did the dance start?"

"The legend or the truth?"

"Let's start with the legend."

"They needed a festival to celebrate the start of the summer. The longer days, the warmer nights, exactly like a thousand other festivals around the country. Very boring."

Jeez. Nobody wanted to make this easy, did they? "That's it? Man, your marketing people sucked. What's the truth, then?"

"A lot better. You remember Walter Willoughby?"

"The railroad tycoon?"

"That's the one. Willoughby kept his mistress upstate, but he didn't have a reason to keep traveling there without his wife, so he bribed the Harmony Springs town council to create the festival. He laid tracks, built the station and greased a whole crew of palms to insure that the festival was a rip-roaring success. Not only did he get to spend time with his mistress, but after the festival took off, he made a fortune. A man's got to admire thinking like that."

"And the wife?"

Stewart grinned, a nice grin, nothing curdled or distracted there. "Actually, she became the wealthy widow. It seems that old Walter had four mistresses in Harmony Springs not just one. And there was hell to pay when they found out about each other. They found Willoughby's body the next day. Drowned, shot, stabbed and poisoned."

Jenn began to smile. "Now I see. That's a good story."

"Willoughby's ancestry disagrees."

"No one likes skeletons. But thank you for telling me."

"You know, the courthouse is supposed to be haunted with his ghost."

"Really?"

He laughed. "Nah. That's just marketing."

"See, you country folks can learn the big bad ways, too."

They danced a couple of dances, and she got some more material, but eventually Stewart noticed her lack of interest and moved on to a twentysomething with a low-cut blouse. At least somebody was getting lucky tonight, she thought, chatting up the bartender, Anisha, who was an Indian girl with some really good jokes, earning extra money on the weekend. Jenn spent some time complaining about men in general, when she sighted the very cause of her complaint.

Aaron. Did wonders never cease? He was sitting at a table in the shadows, alone, no surprise there, drinking a can of what looked to be diet soda. She would have pegged him for a Scotch drinker, not zero calories, no caffeine, but since she would have bet her last dollar he wouldn't have shown up at a dance, her inductive reasoning wasn't as sharp as it usually was.

Or maybe he came to see her?

Tonight he was dressed in funeral black, looking very spiffy except for the trademarked scowl on his face. The black shirt looked vaguely European, accentuating his rangy build, and his hair had been combed in an orderly fashion. She had a devious urge to go over and mess it up, just because it seemed out of place.

However, there were many schools of thought in relationship management which instructed the female to stay aloof and not look so needy.

On the other hand, Aaron seemed not to be a believer in those schools—or any schools of relationship management—and Jenn had always sucked at school anyway.

Trying not to look too desperate, she sauntered over, sat down across from him, and wiggled her fingers in a provocative wave.

"Thank you for the towels," she started off.

"What towels?" he asked, playing innocent, a novel role for Aaron. But—no surprise at all—he didn't do it well.

"Do not be coy with me. I know you left them. Take credit for something good. You deserve it."

"You're welcome," he said, sounding surly instead of courteous, and then sat silent and even surlier.

It was a good thing that perseverance was Jenn's middle name. Actually it was Prudence, but Jenn thought Perseverance suited her better, and she tried again. "I didn't expect to see you here. I wouldn't think that a quaint town dance is your idea of an exciting Friday night."

"I live to surprise you," he answered, sounding more like himself.

"How's the writing coming along? Killed off any females lately?"

"No. Why do you ask?"

Jenn took a sip from her wine and shrugged. "Making polite conversation. There is no subversive motive."

"I usually assume the worst in people. I'm usually right."

"I would've assumed you wouldn't get rid of a snake. I would be wrong. I wouldn't have assumed you would put two very sumptuous towels on my doorstep. I would be wrong. Assumptions are dangerous things. Facts are what matters. You have to stick with the facts."

"I would assume you're here to annoy me. Would I be wrong?"

She sat back in her chair, studied the tension in his face, the caution in his eyes. He wasn't happy, but he was here. "You're very tricky."

"How so?"

"You don't really assume I'm here to annoy you. Actually, you assume I'm sitting here because I want to sleep with you again, but you don't want to ask that, because that would imply that you care if I want to sleep with you again, and you don't want me to know you care."

His mouth twisted in that oddly charming manner of his. She knew it was supposed to be sarcastic and forbidding, but it didn't match the warm light in his eyes.

"You're on your fifth glass of wine, aren't you? Only alcohol should be responsible for logic that twisted."

"Insulting me only proves my point further," she stated confidently.

Whenever he smiled at her with that uncomfortable curve to his mouth, she felt a little tipsy. Sadly, diet soda did not cause tipsy, only punch-drunk lust. "Why are you here? To annoy me?" he asked.

She leaned in, living dangerously, flaunting dangerously, and not really caring, because she desperately wanted to sleep with him again. Properly. With full coital joining and a mutual sharing of orgasms. The way the rest of the world did it. The way that involved personal connections. Those very connections that he shunned.

"I'm here because I'm attracted to you. Your naked body. Your twisted mind. Do you care?" she added in a mocking voice.

But he surprised her once again. "I care. Do you want to dance?"

The shock of it numbed her normally instinctual need to delve further. "Do you dance?" she asked instead, which was much more innocent, and much less dangerous. A woman could live on the edge for only so long.

"You believe I don't dance? Another assumption?"

Now she had a chance to fully recover and she was ready this time. "Nope. I just said it to annoy you. You are so much fun to annoy. Your mouth sets into this grim reaper smile and your eyes narrow to slits."

He grabbed her hand and led her out to the floor, and his eyes were not narrowed, and his mouth was set into something that almost resembled a smile.

7

AARON EXCELLED AT the waltz. Jenn had never waltzed in her life, but he was surprisingly patient, not swearing too loudly when she trounced on his toes, and eventually she got the hang of it.

"Who taught you to dance?"

"A female friend of my father's. His set was a great believer in the odd and the eccentric."

"It explains much," she noted, but she kept her voice nice and gentle and noncombative.

When the crowd started getting too dense, he took her hand and led her outside, wandering down the primrose path, meandering close to the lake. Some people who were not attuned to the intricate workings of his mind might have considered it romantic.

Jenn knew better than to believe that. Although secretly she hoped.

Gas lanterns flickered with light. Possibly environmentally irresponsible, but pretty nonetheless. Aaron walked slowly with all the relaxed temperament of a man grown apart from the city.

"Why did you want to be a writer?" she asked, not that she was surprised at his choice, but it was unconventional, it was radical, it spoke of a man who listened to no one but himself.

He paused for a moment, and stared out over the quiet waters of the lake. "My father considered himself a great literary genius. An undiscovered talent who was passed over by publishing bean counters because of their vacuous tastes for monetized drivel. He always said he didn't care, but then he'd go through the bookstores, thumbing through titles and making fun of everything there. It ruined his life. He wanted to be recognized. He hated that he wasn't. And he hated that he cared." His voice held the disdain of a man who despised the obsession. Fascinating.

"And you chose writing because?"

Aaron shrugged, his eyes fixed somewhere beyond the present. "I don't know."

"Can I ask you a personal question?"

"Now you think about respecting personal boundaries? Go ahead."

"How can you afford not to work?"

At her question, his shoulders hunched tight and tense, and his eyes grew cool and aloof. "About eight years ago I got lucky and came into some money. It's enough to keep me in my cabin in the woods."

"What happens when the money goes? What will you do then?"

"Be poor," he stated, sounding cavalier about the possibility. It was only rich people who thought like that. Poor people knew that being poor sucked.

"Why not do something else?" she asked, sounding exactly like her mother, but there was a certain wisdom in planning for a rainy day. Since they were talking about someone other than herself, she felt especially curious.

The north shore of the lake was far away from the tiny campground with its rustic amenities. Here where they walked, a line of stately houses, built in a time long past, watched over the water. It was easy to walk here and dream.

"Would you do something else?" he said, shooting many holes through her shining moment of sounding responsible, and he didn't even look sad about it.

"I'm not ready to abandon my ship yet. But I have memorized too many of my parents' lectures not to think about the problems of an unreliable career path."

"You'll be fine," he assured her, which both surprised and pleased her, the best of both worlds, in Jenn's opinion.

"Why?" she asked, shamelessly fishing for compliments.

"Because being a journalist is who you are. You might end up waiting tables in a restaurant, or you might end up driving a cab, but you'll be back writing articles and sniffing into other people's lives and tempting them to tell you all sorts of things that they don't want to tell you, and shouldn't tell you if they were smart. But you'll end up there because it's you."

She envied his calm acceptance of the world. No, it wasn't idealistic or happy, but it didn't worry him. Jenn felt permanently unsettled, and she'd never really thought of how much she yearned to be calm.

There was a row of dandelions along the dirt path, and she plucked one, puffing away at the tiny fluff, watching how it fell apart and scattered to unchartered lands.

"I do love your cheerful take on life," she told him, possibly sarcastically, but he seemed to understand that best.

"And thus, my literary success to date."

There was a certain forbidden magic in the night. A certain weight of anticipation in the air, the coming storm. In the distance, thunder rumbled, low and quiet. The lake water lapped against the shore, slow and steady, matching the drumming in Jennifer's blood.

"There's the house where Willoughby was murdered," he told her, pointing to a narrow Victorian with the lights on in the upstairs.

"Stewart said it wasn't haunted."

"It's not. I thought you might want to see it."

"Why are you doing this?" she asked, not so sarcastic this time.

"Doing what?"

"Being here. With me."

"Am I with you?" he asked, more of those diversionary questions designed to give nothing away. Tired of the games, Jenn headed for people of a less difficult persuasion. But before she could move away, he stopped her with a persevering hand to her arm. "Jennifer. Don't. I'm sorry. You want to know why I like you?"

"Yes."

"I have a typewriter, a one-eyed cat with a personality disorder and a window that looks out over the dark side of the lake. The rest of my life exists inside my head. For a long time, I was in love with that life, but not so much anymore. I don't know if I got older, lonelier or wiser, but something is different. Most people I still don't like. You, I like."

Such simple words to cause such a nonsimple thrill.

"Why?"

"Are you going to make me spout poetry?"

"Do you spout poetry?"

"Not when sober."

"Then, no, I'm not going to make you spout poetry. Why do you like me?"

He stopped walking, looked at her sideways.

"Besides your ass?"

"Now you're teasing me."

"No. I actually do like your ass. It's very curvy."

Mostly due to an unhealthy dependency on sugar, but she chose not to tell him that. "Besides that."

"Your luscious breasts. Very soft and touchable."

"Besides that."

"I like your mouth," he said, stroking a finger over her lips, which shuddered. She closed her eyes, craving this one gentle touch more than she wanted anything before.

"It's soft and touchable, too," he continued. "But not sweet. Sharp. Tangy."

She felt his mouth on hers, another gentle touch. Seductive.

When he lifted his head, she opened her eyes and saw the pale fires there, carefully banked. He was asking. Unlike other men, Aaron was careful never to take.

"I like your mouth, too," she whispered.

"I like your eyes," he told her, as if admitting the world's greatest sin.

"Really? Why?"

His mouth twisted into a reluctant smile. He was getting better at that, she noticed. "You do like your compliments, don't you?"

"We all like our compliments. Tell me. For a man of words, you don't use enough."

"You won't kiss me again until I do?" he asked, his large palm cupping her cheek, carefully and perfectly controlled.

"I might kiss you again, but I'll do more if you'll tell me why you like my eyes."

"Don't you think that's demeaning? Reducing all your positive characteristics to the physical?"

"Can I tell you a secret?"

"I don't believe you keep a secret if your life depended on it."

He had no idea of the secrets she was keeping from him. The heavy thump-thump of her heart when he touched her. The sharp thrill she felt when he looked at her. The dreams in her head of him filling her, joining her, being a part of her.

"What secret," he prodded, apparently more curious than he cared to admit.

"I don't care much about the compliments. I just like to watch you think, the way you frown, carefully constructing the perfect turn of phrase. You torture yourself."

He frowned at her, but she suspected it was for the effect. "You have a very twisted mind. And that, my darling distraction, is why I like you."

"Are you going to kiss me again?"

"If you ask nicely."

He stood and kissed her slowly. She put a hand over his heart, feeling the racing beat, and she smiled, content to stand there, tasting his mouth. So many times in her life, she wanted to be somewhere else, but not now. Now she wanted to be here. Now she wanted this.

Her hands wound around his waist, binding him to her. His hips pulsed against hers, hard, urgent, and she sighed into his mouth. Carefully, so slight that he shouldn't notice, she curved into his erection, but he unfused his mouth from hers, and took a step back.

But there was something new in his eyes. Intent. A promise. Feeling remarkably calm, Jennifer smiled.

He sat down in the grass and held out his hand.

"You're making me nervous here. What sorts of creatures lurk in the woods?" she asked, sitting next to him, leaning back on her hands, an open invitation for whatever creature was lurking nearby. Or whatever man was lurking, as well.

He didn't want—he pounced.

This time, his kiss wasn't easy or soft or simple. This kiss was like the man. Complicated. Confusing. Intoxicating. His tongue stroked back and forth, and in less than a beat, her tongue mingled with his, following his lead.

His hands grasped her face, and she knew there would be marks, but she didn't care. Finally he was letting go. It was a heady feeling being ferociously explored, being absolutely desired. She was his albatross, his white whale, his magnificent obsession.

Yes, the story was going to end badly. When she left this place, she would delude herself into thinking that he would call, and it would hurt when he didn't. It should have been enough to keep her away, but after years of mistakes, of choosing unwisely, Jenn wanted to have a heart-pounding affair with someone who didn't shoplift, who didn't watch cartoons, who spent his days using his mind. It made her blood heat, her vision hazy and not so sharp, and her thighs shiftless and willing.

She lay back in the grass, winding her arms around his neck, tangling her fingers in his silky hair, pulling him down on top of her because she knew he would do it right. Already her body was curving into his, and her hips were rolling up, mating there. There was no uncertainty, no experimentation. This was animal attraction at its finest. This would be sex at its finest. Hopefully tomorrow there would be no regrets. "Be with me," she asked.

Sure and sly, his hand slid beneath her shirt, her bra, unerringly finding her breast. He rolled her nipple between his finger and thumb, discovering the perfect amount of pressure that Jenn could endure. *Exactly that,* she thought with a gasp, nipping at his neck, pleased with the catch of his own breath.

Cleverly his hands moved over her, sliding up her shirt. The night breeze spilled over her skin, and she realized she was developing a grand passion for the great outdoors. It felt warm and wicked, or maybe that was the wicked feel of this man and what she knew was to come.

Definitely the man, she thought, when his mouth closed over her breast. Oh, yes. Above her, the sky was filled with a moon and shooting stars, or maybe that was in her head. And the music, the thundering pulse in her skin, that must be in her head, as well. The deep pulls of his mouth were making her mind fall apart.

Her fingers dug into the hard ridges of his back, the merging of spine and sinew and skin. Nothing he did was easy, his hips grinding into hers, and she could feel the thick bulge of his cock pressing between her thighs. Not happy about the layers between them, her hands moved to his fly, wanting to feel skin, wanting to feel Aaron, wanting to feel cock. She usually didn't feel so hungry, so impatient, so desperate for sex, but her body was already primed for him, and she couldn't wait.

At the touch of her hand, he raised his head, his eyes meeting hers, glittering in the dark. "You're sure about this."

In answer, she unzipped his fly, pulling him free.

His breath exploded before he yanked down her jeans, her panties, making her smile. Yeah, she wasn't the only one feeling the heat.

The smile froze when he pushed inside her, and Jenn felt her entire body contract around him. Her thighs, her skin, her blood, her mind. The perfect connection. For a single second he was still, poised over her, his eyes closed tight as if he was in pain, but then he exhaled and began to move.

Quickly she realized her mistake. This wasn't sex—this was death by possession. Oh, sweet mother, yes. He was thick and hard and each time he shoved into her, she could feel her body shudder. He took her mouth, his tongue pressing deep.

Oh, yes.

There was something so basic and primitive about him, about this. About her back scraping against the hard ground, about her pants twisted around her ankles, about the sharp lines of desire in his face.

Her hands pulled at the grass, wanting to keep still, but unable. His hips drove her forward, pushing her upward, tearing her apart, and she felt like she was flying, being swept up to some distant world of pleasure.

He ripped his mouth from hers, buried his face in her neck. When he spoke, his voice was quaking with pain, with fear, with desire. "I'm...hurting you."

You will, she thought. But not here. She loved this brutalness to him, this raw honesty. This was what she had known was inside him. She loved the driving force between her thighs, feeling his muscles bunch and pull and feeling his breath come so quick and ragged.

She pressed her lips against his hair, thinking he wouldn't notice, thinking he wouldn't care. Immediately he froze, his cock embedded deep inside her. Sex, she reminded herself. Sex. It would be easier if he didn't look at her like that. Shock, nerves, fear. "Say something," he muttered. "Say this is okay."

"It's more than okay," she whispered, almost a prayer. "It's very, very good."

IT WAS HELL. IT WAS the worst sort of hell. Aaron didn't want this.

She was leaving him.

He kept chanting that safe refrain in his mind, but every time he moved inside her, she surrounded him, clung to him, keeping him there in that place he longed to be. He was moored to her, chained to her, locked to her.

He didn't want this to be so good, so golden, so her.

With each thrust, everything shifted inside him, all the false hopes and old pleas rising in his throat like bile, but it didn't matter.

For the moment he lived in this dream, he belonged in this dream. He belonged in her.

She was leaving him, he repeated, but his mind didn't listen. Not now. Tomorrow he would be back in control, but for now, he lost himself all over again.

SHE SPENT THE NIGHT AT his cabin. There was grass in her hair, stains on her jeans, her cute pin-striped, button-down shirt would never be wearable again, and there was a long bruise that ran down her thigh.

It was impossible to stop grinning.

Oh, Jenn knew the warning signs. Stupid girl falling for ass-hat treatment because man acts lonely and has tormented bedroom eyes that appeal to her. Then stupid girl throws away her pride somewhere after the bra and before the panties. But she couldn't stop herself from wanting him, anymore than she could stop breathing, or completing her life-or-death quest for the perfect cup of coffee.

Aaron's cabin had surprised her. After seeing the rustic and inhumane design scheme of hers, she assumed they were all like that. She'd been wrong. He had a mountain of a bed, with a pillow-top mattress that promised great sex, great sleep and zero back pains in the morning.

Feeling marvelously alive, she stretched against the soft mattress and purred; there was no other word for the rumble that emerged from her throat. "You live nicely," she told him, wondering why he was so far away. There was a scratched and scuffed dining table, a maze of bookcases that seemed to tile almost precariously and a dorm-size refrigerator tucked in the corner, almost as an afterthought.

"Good morning," he said easily, politely, distantly. And they were back to square one. She ignored the fleeting hurt in her heart, and her easy, polite and not remotely distant smile stayed firmly fixed on her face.

A large gray cat perched atop the overstuffed book-shelves, watching her with one blind eye, one malevolent one, and a snarl that matched Aaron's.

"That's the cat?"

"That's Two."

"Two cats?" she asked, blinking to check her eyes.

"His name is Two."

"Why?"

"One ran away."

"Your first cat, that I assume you named One?"

"You assume correctly."

"Creative and imaginative," she said. The cat growled, low in his throat, and she wasn't sure if the creature was insulted or jealous.

"He likes tuna fish and has a general hatred for people."

"Except for you?"

"Including me. He only tolerates me because I feed him."

"I don't know. I think that's affection in one of his eyes."

"That's the blind one."

"What do you write?"

"Fiction."

She rolled on her stomach, dangling her feet in the air, watching his eyes follow the line of her skin, and she knew he was thinking about sex. Some of the hurt disappeared. "I know that, but what sort of fiction? Mysteries with lots of blood and crazed killers that think of new and painful ways to torture? Adventure books with a cynical spy who seduces women at will?"

He shook his head, and his normally cool eyes were amused. "Postapocalyptical fiction. The general desolation of a barren landscape, a world sucked dry from the greed and brutality of civilization. And the small band of survivors forced to work together or die."

"I should have guessed that one."

For a few minutes he watched her, and it was like a fire on her skin. She could see how much he wanted her. See the way his fingers drummed on his leg. It was a heady feeling, but the leash was firmly back in place.

"What did this to you?" she asked.

"What do you mean?"

"Oh, don't get stupid now. Everything around you is dark and lonely. You've picked this place on purpose. It's not by chance. Why?"

"My surroundings enhance my work," he said with that absolute certainty that always rings false. As a professional self-doubter, Jenn knew the truth.

"What if that's not the point? What if all this is a single voice in the wilderness, the mournful cry of a man who hates to be alone?"

"If that were true, I'd be very stupid."

"Or stubborn," she insisted.

"That would be what a woman would want to see. But it wouldn't be real," he reminded her.

"So, who did this to you?"

"I was born like this. You were born to poke your nose into other people's lives. I was born to live alone."

"Except for the cat," she pointed out.

"Don't read too much into it. He found me."

"Where's the typewriter?"

"What typewriter?" he asked, looking so innocent, so clueless, so terribly endearing because she knew he was lying his ass off, and frankly, he didn't do it well. His eyes shifted to the floor, dodging her eyes as well as her question.

"The typewriter you brutalize every night. I can hear you."

She thought he was going to lie to her again, but then he met her not-going-to-fool-me eyes, and shrugged. "It's under the bed."

Carefully she reached a hand under the wooden bed frame, touched the cold steel and smiled. "When I was a kid, I thought there were alligators under my bed. Some people think there are ghosts and vampires that live there."

He looked at her, shocked. "My typewriter is not some figment of nightmares. I put it there because I'm tidy."

Jenn scanned the room, the inches of dust on the books, the mangled white balls that covered the floor. "Not that tidy," she corrected. "Why do you hide it?"

"When will you stop asking questions?"

"When I'm no longer interested."

"The apocalypse won't be here soon enough."

"Don't be melodramatic. Last night was pretty awesome."

When he looked at her with that hungry intensity, she could feel her mouth go dry, and she knew his look was mirrored in her eyes. She wanted him not to be a mistake, not be a diversion, but every inch of her knew that was wrong. Why did parents always have to be right?

He smiled at her, slow and sad. "She longed for a world where justice reigned, where goodness lived, where music played sweetly in the night. Desperately she believed in things that were not, in hearts long shipwrecked, in blind eyes that pierced the light. In the end, the world was not hers to rule, and heartbroken, she wandered an endless path, finding no peace in her madness."

Jenn frowned, not sure whether she'd been complimented or insulted or both. "Who said that?"

"I did."

Certainly she was no expert, but she recognized his talent for what it was. "You're wasting yourself here."

He nodded without modesty. "Probably."

And that was the end of the discussion. That was the way he wanted it, and he would sit in the woods forever. Alone. And the world would never know. It was a crime. She sat up and curled her legs beneath her. "Finish the story, Aaron. You want to. It's there in your face. It's the bitch that won't let you go."

"Do your job, Jennifer. Write your story, go away. Go explore the world and leave me in peace."

It was the very worst thing he could say, reminding her of the smarter choice, but he didn't know that. Or maybe he did. He'd just told her that she believed in what was not, in what could not be, and it was just the way she was. Her very own Twinkie defense.

Moved by those very beliefs she couldn't set aside, she went to him and pressed her lips to his throat. "This is peace."

"No. It's hell."

But his voice was broken, and his hands pulled her close. Under her hand, his shipwrecked heart raced. It was the best sort of hell.

LATER THAT MORNING, THERE was coffee. Full-bodied, robust coffee with a bold, eye-awakening aroma and the tiniest hint of spice. Jenn's nose quivered at the scent, already tasting the smooth flavors on her tongue.

"Please tell me I'm not dreaming," she breathed, shamelessly seduced.

"You're not dreaming." He handed a cup to her.

Not trusting him, she took a sip, savoring the ambrosia and the mind-popping caffeine. "It's perfect. How did you make this?"

"Fresh-ground beans and a coffeepot on the grill."

He answered so easily as if everyone went though all that work for a cup of coffee. "It's delicious."

"Thank you."

"Have you ever considered a coffeemaker?" she asked, needing to point out that technology had advanced beyond the Stone Age. Now they had the wheel, fire and a strange contraption known as the automobile.

His grunt echoed from a time when Neanderthals roamed the earth. "The flavor isn't as good from a coffeemaker. It's homogenized, artificial."

She took another sip, breathed in the nectar of the coffee gods, and sighed with delight. "Okay, it's a heck of a lot of work, but it's good."

"Sometimes easy isn't always the best."

The master of the implied metaphor. She looked him over, and smiled. "No. I guess not."

He crossed his legs, a curiously protective gesture. "When are you leaving?"

Okay, that was sudden. Jenn scanned for her clothes,

the bra, the one missing shoe. "Leaving for New York?" she prattled, making polite conversation while she got out of his hair as quickly as possible.

"Leaving for downtown Harmony Springs," he clarified, which was better, but not by much.

She pulled her shirt over her head, not bothering with a bra. "I didn't realize I was an imposition."

"A distraction," he corrected, his gaze fixed on her chest, which made her feel somewhat better, although it still meant he wanted her gone. No, he thought this would break her, but he was wrong. Jenn had survived missteps over and over again.

After she tugged on her sandals, she smoothed her hair into something less tangled. "I'm going to interview the mayor." Hopefully he'd have something good, something interesting, something that would keep her job. Usually Jenn was a little more focused than this, a little less... distracted.

She looked at the cause of her distraction and frowned. He stood all the way across the room, as far from her as humanly possible, but the distance never mattered. Sex hadn't made it better, only worse. The pull between them hung in the air, as constant as the moon's pull on the tides. She could feel it and he could, as well.

"Come down later. I'll make dinner," he offered.

Dinner? That was new, that was different. That was progress, she whispered to herself. No, she argued back. He probably wanted to watch her eat, so the next day he would use the details when he poisoned her in his book.

"You'll hunt it, skin it, roast it over the fire?" she asked, trying to make a joke, needing to clear the fragile hopes from her mind.

He grinned at her, and fragile hopes bloomed anew. Much like weeds. "Takeout. There's a great American

GET 2 BOOK

We'd like to send you two *Harlequin® Blaze™* novels absolutely free. Accepting them puts you under no obligation to purchase any more books.

HOW TO GET YOUR
2 FREE BOOKS AND 2 FREE GIFTS

1. Return the reply card today, and we'll send you two *Harlequin Blaze* novels, absolutely free! We'll even pay the postage!

2. Accepting free books places you under no obligation to buy anything, ever. Whatever you decide, the free books and gifts are yours to keep, free!

3. We hope that after receiving your free books you'll want to remain a subscriber, but the choice is yours—to continue or cancel, any time at all!

EXTRA BONUS

You'll also get two free mystery gifts! (worth about $10)

FREE!

If offer card is missing, write to The Reader Service, P.O. Box 1867, Buffalo, NY 14240-1867 or visit www.ReaderService.com

BUSINESS REPLY MAIL

FIRST-CLASS MAIL   PERMIT NO. 717   BUFFALO, NY

POSTAGE WILL BE PAID BY ADDRESSEE

**THE READER SERVICE
PO BOX 1867
BUFFALO NY 14240-9952**

NO POSTAGE
NECESSARY
IF MAILED
IN THE
UNITED STATES

fusion place about a mile north of here. I'm not the complete Neanderthal you think I am."

Right.

DINNER WAS AS GOOD as Aaron had hoped. He'd bluffed about the restaurant. Yes, he'd read about it, heard Carolyn gush about it, but he'd never eaten there. He didn't need ornately presented meals, or delicate sauces or quiet companionship, but when Jenn studied him, her eyes were unflinching, and yet still welcoming. He realized how isolated he'd become. Since he'd been in Harmony Springs, he'd forgotten what music sounded like, he'd forgotten how food could taste, he'd forgotten all those quiet details of life that were starting to come back.

She had a way of getting to him, getting beneath his skin. There was a sharpness to her, a determination that he respected and understood. But when he talked to her, he could *feel her,* as well. Feel her emotions seeping into him. Aaron liked being the clear-eyed narrator in his own life, grasping the truth in human nature in all its selfish misery. He knew that when feelings boiled to the surface, some of that unvarnished honesty disappeared, and got lost in the mix.

"How's the article coming?" he asked, watching as she scooped the last bits of her chocolate mousse.

"Not well enough."

"What's wrong?"

"You promise not to laugh?" she asked, but she didn't mind being laughed at. He knew that now. She made fun of herself as naturally as she took a breath, but it wasn't to put herself down. Jenn was happy, and she didn't care.

"No," he teased, pleased to see her smile, but it disappeared too soon.

"They're cutting staff. My job's on the line. Lizette and

I are fighting for one position. She's winning. She's got the scoop on the councilman who was just indicted for construction kickbacks. She's also sleeping with our boss."

"Oh."

"I can't compete."

"Yes you can," he encouraged, foolish words that had no basis in reality. He only wanted to make her feel better. No story on Harmony Springs was going to beat one on corruption and scandal. It was the dirty laundry that fed the news. It was the sordid dishonesty that people ate up in droves. He could look at his royalty statements, and know that nothing titillated the public's appetite like the great flaws of mankind.

"How am I supposed to do that?"

"With your writing."

"There's no story here. There's no late-breaking headlines up here."

Yes, there were. She had no idea what was here, and it made him uncomfortable, made him guilty enough to want to correct her, want to spew out his life story in full three-column, above-the-fold details, but he didn't. At the end of the day, at the end of two weeks, Jennifer Dade would go home, return to the city where she belonged, and Aaron would be back to where he started.

In the end, he protected himself and his work above all. Jenn would land on her feet. He could even help her. That thought made him feel proud and noble, generous. Human. "I could help you."

"How?"

"There's lot of things to write about. The abandoned sanitarium with the tunnels underneath. Isaiah's Purple Heart that he won in Korea, or the Summer Festival. It's all here."

"Do you think that's enough? It doesn't sound like much."

No, it probably wasn't enough, but there were other things, too, he told himself gallantly. Pieces that only he knew. The dark secrets of the area.

For the next week, Aaron would risk Didi's wrath and not worry about his writing. He would show Jennifer the town of Harmony Springs through unvarnished eyes. Hopefully there was enough material to keep her employed. Not that he was sure the material mattered. If her editor was sleeping with the other reporter, the decision might have already been made. Aaron knew that men could be bought off easily with sex. They could twist their principles into convoluted knots. And when great sex was involved, they could puff themselves up with self-importance and nobility. With the promise of a willing body underneath them, they suffered from delusions of grandeur and could be diverted from almost anything that was honest and true.

The great flaws of mankind. Sometimes fiction came from life, and sometimes—in a great screw of fate—life imitated fiction.

THE NEXT MORNING, JENNIFER returned to her cabin, and there was a box outside her door. A very prosaic, cardboard box with a blue polka-dot bow. Instantly she attacked it.

Inside the box was a coffeemaker, some filters, a bean-grinder and a bag of dark roast Colombian beans. Giddy with excitement, she tore open the bag and inhaled, the magical aroma seeping into her senses.

It was a good ten minutes before the initial euphoria was over. Jenn moved the packages inside and laid them out in a line, debating the meaning behind the gift. She knew Aaron had given it to her. She knew playing Santa Claus didn't come easily to him. So, either a) he wanted something from her and was using bribery to get it, or b) he wanted to please her. She considered the implications of the first, but knew there wasn't anything he could want from her that she hadn't already given or was willing to give. Which left option B. He wanted to please her.

She hugged the coffee filters close to her heart and somewhere in the woods, the crickets began to sing.

Yes, he frustrated her, he infuriated her, he baffled her. But in spite of all that, she liked the burly edges to him, the socially awkward behavior, the hungry way he watched her when she was getting undressed, the dark light in his eyes when he moved inside her. All these things pleased her, but the coffeemaker touched her in other places. It wedged into the tiny cracks behind the intellect of her mind. It wiggled its way into little hollows that were precariously close to her heart.

Before this considerate gesture, she'd planned on going to town, planned on hitting the pavement in search of some angle for her article to achieve better job security, but now she wanted to say thank you. She wanted to watch the reaction on his face. Maybe see some flickering of feeling for her. *Maybe,* she thought.

Yes, Jenn was smart and wise in the ways of temporary men, and yes, she hadn't considered anything beyond two weeks. Certainly he wasn't the sort who did anything more than two weeks…but the idea of something more brought an idealistic smile to her face. The very sort of dreamy hopefulness that her parents had said had landed her with a Masters of Arts degree and a haphazard outlook on life.

As she ran toward his cabin, she nearly tripped over a rock, but she recovered her balance and slowed her pace. After she regained her composure and her breath, she smoothed her hair and rubbed her damp palms on her shorts.

The sounds of war were coming from his cabin; the typewriter was being pummeled. Aaron was hard at work, and would probably hate being disturbed.

She knocked.

"Go away."

"It's Jennifer."

There was a long silence, not the breathless race to the door she had imagined.

Eventually the door creaked open. "What?" he asked. Again, not the giddy can't-wait-to-see-you-again she had imagined, but still, he'd opened the door. That counted.

"Thank you for the coffeemaker."

"You're welcome," he said, and then slammed the door in her face.

Instantly the typing started.

Once again, Jenn knocked on the door.

Silence.

Eventually he opened it, after her knocking wore him down. "I said thank you," she repeated.

"I know. I said you're welcome."

She peeked around him, staring at the inside of his cabin. It was a disaster. Paper balls littered the floor like a carpet, and Two was batting them around.

"You're working," she announced stupidly, wishing he could make this easier on her.

"You should be working, too," he reminded her.

It finally dawned on her that she shouldn't have come. She shouldn't have thanked him. She shouldn't have expected abrupt personality changes, and most of all, she shouldn't care. "I didn't mean to disturb you."

She turned to go, not nearly so cheerful anymore, cursing her parents, cursing her poor career choices, cursing her poor men choices, and in general, cursing anybody that was happier than she was at the moment.

"Jennifer," he called after her, but this time she was smarter and left. It was a lot better to hide her disappointment, to hide the hurt. He already thought she was gullible and foolish. Better to leave some doubt in the matter.

"Jennifer?"

The terra firma of the forest snapped as he walked, so many living things breaking underneath his feet. The noise was a sharp reminder that although Aaron was a great lover and could seduce her mind and her body at will, he was also exceptionally talented at destroying things. "Wait."

She stayed where she was, and sniffed delicately, solely to indicate her displeasure.

"I'm sorry. I was working," he said.

Working? Was that what he called the hundreds of crumpled pages on the floor? "You were killing trees," she argued, admiring his dedication and resenting it, as well.

"I'm killing trees one large forest at a time," he said, and his voice was very soft and very gentle making it very hard to remain unmoved.

"I'm glad you liked the coffeemaker," he said simply, followed by nothing by silence. No sentimental "thinking of you," no flowery "I wanted to make you smile."

"Is that all?" she asked, knowing that she should have held her tongue, but she wanted a little more. She wanted to know that she was unsettling his life as much as he was unsettling hers. It seemed only fair.

Instead of looking unsettled, he looked at her, eyes puzzled. "I think that's all. Shouldn't that be all?"

Pasting an understanding smile on her face, Jenn pushed a hand through her hair. Inside her mind, her rational self patiently explained to her emotional self that Aaron was not Lord Byron nor was he remotely emo. He didn't spend his hours contemplating the wonderfulness of her, and conversely he wouldn't understand why a woman would want to interrupt his work in order to spend a few more seconds in his not-so-comfortable company. It was that absolute lack of basic human norms that touched her so deeply. "You're right," she told him.

Slowly he took her hand, his fingers clasping and unclasping on hers, looking almost unsettled. "I don't do this well. It's why I'm in the middle of nowhere, alone with my cat, because I usually end up pissing people off. I don't want to piss you off. I'm sorry."

Her rational self studied him, saw the hard detachment in his eyes, saw the brittle tension in his shoulders and knew that Aaron Smith stayed alone in his world, and that was the way he wanted it. But her emotional self, that one that wasn't quite so logical, noticed he held on to her hand a little too long, a little too urgently, and a little too much like a man who didn't want to let go.

For now, it was enough, and Jenn walked away with a smile.

8

IT WAS A HOUSE THAT had been both heaven and hell. Aaron had returned to Harmony Springs to prove to himself that it didn't matter, that he could live within a memory's reach and yet never return to his old life again.

Until now.

The old mansion stood high on the hill, as lofty as the occupants that had once lived there. Now the sunlight was not so kind. The paint was peeling, the hedges were overgrown and there was an old Beware Of Dog sign that had been posted for over thirty years. The sign had been Aaron's inspiration. The others had laughed as if he was the most clever boy.

Jennifer held his hand as they walked around the deserted grounds. He noticed that she often held his hand as if she enjoyed touching him, as if she needed to touch him. Often he would touch her, as well. He told himself it was because she expected it and not for his desires. It was a good lie and served his mind well.

"What is this place?" she asked, leaning against the white picket fence, where the roses had once bloomed.

"It's the summer home of Lillian Bose."

"The writer? I didn't know she had a place up here."

"She used to host these literary salons, and she and her friends would sit for days dissecting a book, a paragraph, a single line, congratulating one another on their own cleverness. An incoherent analysis of Faulkner or a loose-tongued critique of *Dubliners*. Every Sunday evening she held a limerick contest. The prize was a bottle of Red Label. The Scotch was the only thing fit for public consumption."

Jennifer walked up on the porch, peeking into the boarded-up windows, her eyes alight with great possibilities. The reality was not nearly so worthy. "Seriously? Literary salons? I never knew all this."

"No one did. It was a big joke among the Ephemera's Lament, that's what they called themselves. The group would come up here during the summer, pull out the port because beer was too bourgeois, and then proceed to outquip each other, dream up new stories, and then, when they were too drunk to stand, they'd have sex with whomever was close."

"How do you know about all this?"

"When you live up here, you learn."

"Do they still have the parties?" she asked, pulling out her phone and taking pictures of the old place.

"After Lillian died, the estate went to her daughter. Her daughter didn't like the group, thought they were morally bankrupt. The salon stopped. A few years ago, the daughter lost everything. I think the state is haggling over back taxes."

"What a crime. It should be a museum or something. There should at least be a plaque."

There was nothing worth remembering of this place, but no matter how he tried, Aaron could still hear the drunken laughter, the jeering commentary and the incessant whine of his own voice. He had ached for his father to approve of him, abating himself to please the unpleasant man. It was a long, long time before Aaron realized his father wasn't worth the pain, but even with that hard-fought knowledge, the pain didn't go away.

Alcohol numbed it, fame had diluted it, a Pulitzer had stopped the flow of arterial blood in it, but even after all the palliative remedies that he'd tried, the need for approval was still there, shivering in the cold corners of his soul. "Martin Turner wrote most of *The Coldest Season* here."

"Get out! I loved that book. Walter was my favorite. It broke my heart when he died at the end. I wanted him to win."

"He was based on the gardener's son," Aaron lied. Actually, Walter had been based on Aaron. "The *Times* came up here in the early seventies to do a profile."

"They knew about it?"

"Hiram Miller, book reporter. He'd gotten a whiff, and wanted to see what it was about. He ended up drunk, naked and photographed in various compromising positions. The article was never written. The world chose to turn its back on the darker side of literary genius."

"I could see that. Any witnesses I can talk to? Something more than vague recollections?"

Aaron looked away from the hopeful light in her eyes. Usually he liked to bask in the luminance, but sometimes, too much light was a bad thing, illuminating shadows that should stay in the dark. He coughed to cover his pause.

"I think most of the parties involved are either dead or would elect not to incriminate themselves, but talk to Mrs. Oliphant who runs the liquor store. She can give you some material. She's old, but she's still got a good memory."

"You're doing this for me? Thank you," she told him, sounding so happy, so grateful, as if he'd done something special just for her. Her eyes watched him as if he'd just handed her the best present yet, and he felt an unfamiliar twinge in his chest. The sort of twinge that reminds a man that he isn't noble or heroic. In the end, he's still the same selfish, self-protective turtle of a man that he'd always been.

When he was little, his imaginary world was a safe haven where he could go in peace. But as he got older, the shell had grown, hardened and turned into the wellspring from where he drew his art.

Back in the day, when his name was whispered with awe and respect, Aaron had prided himself on being as big and arrogant a bastard as his father. He acted without guilt or conscience because people knew Aaron and expected no less.

But Jennifer expected more from him, a hell of a lot more than he was capable of giving. Sometimes at night, when she was asleep in his arms, he dreamed and he wanted to be that man that she imagined him to be.

Because he wanted to make her happy, he pulled her into his arms and pressed his face to her hair. When they were alone together, he almost believed in the happy endings she sought.

THAT NIGHT THEY ORDERED Chinese. He argued that MSG wasn't healthy, but she hiked up the rock to the one shining spot where she could get a cell phone signal, then found a restaurant that was MSG-free. Aaron assumed the restaurant was lying, and Jenn finally convinced him when she explained that the real world was a much nicer place than the wasteland in his stories.

They ate in his cabin, and he told her about the summer of 1990, when Ephemera's Lament had adopted a puppy because they wanted to contrast the pointless life of a dog to the pointlessness of man. When he talked about those days, he never expressed happiness or sadness or anger or any emotion at all. There was no affection, no respect, no sense of presence, even though he had obviously been there. Another person might have colored the stories, exaggerated them for dramatic effect, but not Aaron. His eyes were carefully flat, and he talked in a narrative that conveyed absolutely nothing.

"What happened to the puppy?" she asked, wondering about the words left unsaid.

"He disappeared three weeks later. Lillian said that he ran away."

"Did anyone look for him?"

"No."

"Why not?"

Idly he picked at his noodles, while at the same time dodging her eyes. "They moved on to other things, horse racing at Sarasota, the physics of a bong and whether they could transform the housemaid into a princess and fool the governor with the charade."

It all sounded like great fodder for her article, but she wasn't interested in that right now. Instead she wanted to dig at the detail that seemed to bother him most. "What was the dog like?"

"Four legs. A tail. Ate."

"Fuzzy?"

"No. It was some beagle mix."

"I like beagles," she told him, wanting him to tell her more.

"It's only a dog."

"Yeah," she answered while she stared at the cat sitting atop the maze of bookcases, swishing his tail. "Why don't you get a dog?"

"Dogs are a pain in the ass," answered the man who spent four hours twice a week chopping up organic ingredients for an ungrateful cat that didn't like to be petted.

She chose to withhold her psychological analysis of this contradiction in terms.

After dinner, she pulled out her computer, worked on a few articles, and let him help her. He liked to help her with her writing, and most of his suggestions were spot on. Perhaps there were people in the world who would refuse help from someone else, choosing to go it alone, and succeed on their own merits. Jennifer was not one of those people who she felt made up extra work for themselves when they could be getting more out of life.

And when she finished her work, one hour earlier than she had hoped, she pulled out a Scrabble game that she'd borrowed from Carolyn in the office.

"Do you play?"

At that, he looked more intrigued, his eyes narrowed. "Why don't we make it interesting?"

"Betting?"

"Possibly."

"For what?"

She could read all sorts of answers in his eyes, but he stayed silent, and she knew that this move was up to her.

"We could play strip Scrabble."

He considered the option, and seemed to find it acceptable.

"All right."

There were problems with the Scrabble pieces. An overabundance of the letters *E* and *N* but Jenn was on the case. Rather than having them draw from the pile, she split up the entire bag of letters, because frankly, rules were for losers. This was cottage-version Scrabble, so they'd use whatever tiles were in the bag. After a few moments she proudly submitted her first word.

E-M-B-I-T-T-E-R-E-D.

She grinned at him. "You owe me a shirt," she said,

and watched with avid eyes while he efficiently pulled his cotton T-shirt over his head, and then stared at her blandly, which took some of the fun out of the game. Still, a shirtless Aaron was a feast for the eyes and she wasn't going to complain.

"Your turn," she told him, and he laid out his letters.

E-N-S-N-A-R-E-D.

"Very clever," she said, leaning over the table, making sure he didn't cheat, because he seemed like the type.

"You owe me a shirt," he pointed out, and yes, she knew that, but she wanted him to say it.

She met his eyes, and her fingers went to her buttons, and slowly she slid them free, one by one, liking the way he watched her, liking the heaviness in the air. With elaborate presentation, worthy of the world's best striptease, she slid one arm free, then another, until she stood there in a white lacy bra, that to be fair, was more revealing than not.

He didn't seem to mind, and at the sharp tension in his face, she felt her body respond, felt her nipples peak. He noticed.

She cleared her throat, focused on the small tiles in front of her, clearing the fog from her vision. Eventually she found a word.

E-N-R-A-P-T-U-R-E-D.

Proud of her efforts, she raised her brows. "Pants, please."

He stood, shucked his pants with the same calm efficiency as before. Okay, not there yet. Still, there was something very vulnerable about a man in plain white briefs. For instance, the heavy bulge that showed through, peeking out the band at his waist. She stared at his cock, stared at his face, and was pleased to see a slow flush before he sat down.

"My turn," he said, rearranging his tiles, pretending complete concentration. She wasn't fooled.

E-N-G-R-O-S-S-E-D.

He stared, smiled slowly, cruelly. "Pants, please."

She unzipped her jeans, pushed them down, not as elegant as going topless, but he didn't mind. The tiny scrap of lace that covered her crotch seemed to be a big hit, and she noticed the way his fingers tightened into fists. Very tense fists.

She sat in her chair, leaned over the table and stuck one finger in her mouth, sucking mildly. His look was not amused.

"Can we play?"

"I thought we were," she answered in transparent white lace and a transparent lack of sexual scruples, looking as innocent as physically possible.

She looked at her letters. Laughed.

E-N-L-A-R-G-E.

"Your underwear is mine, mister," she bragged, leaning back in the chair, feeling more confident than she should.

Instead of standing, he bent down and removed one white athletic sock, waving it like a flag. "Not yet."

"Spoilsport," she muttered, and Two, not liking the tone, hissed from above.

He laid out his letters on the little wooden tray.

E-N-S-L-A-V-E-D.

He raised a brow. "Do you have socks? Oops. Now, if had you dressed with more practical footwear, you might be feeling a little less naked."

She glared at him, and removed her bra with more malice than seduction. There was a nice moment when she saw him swallow at the sight of her bare breasts. Feeling spiteful, she brushed at one heavily aroused nipple, clearing away a not-so-imaginary speck of devilment. Aaron stared, heavy lidded, and she politely refrained from peeking under the table. The man was on his last legs. She knew, he knew it. The American people knew it.

She picked at the tiles and fluffed at her hair, before laying them out.

E-N-D-E-A-R-I-N-G.

"If you were a brave man, you wouldn't worry about that extra sock."

He didn't answer, but took off his second sock and gazed impassively.

She locked her thighs together and shifted in her seat.

E-M-B-U-G-G-E-R.

She looked at the letters and frowned. "I don't think that's a word."

"Marquis de Sade, eighteenth century. To bugger. There's an *OED* in the corner. You can look it up."

Feeling more than a little miffed, she stood up, shucked the last scrap of silk and sighed. "You win," she pronounced, never having claimed to be a gracious loser.

"You still have more tiles."

"Look at me," she protested, casting her hand down her body in case he missed that fact. "I don't have anything left to lose."

He sat, silent and thoughtful. "There are options," he finally said, at last getting into the spirit of what strip Scrabble was supposed to be about.

Somewhat mollified, she sat down, squirmed in her seat, realizing that perhaps there was something arousing about playing Scrabble in the nude.

E-N-T-R-E-Z V-O-U-S.

She shot him a flat look, daring him to protest.

He cleared his throat. "Foreign is allowed?" he asked.

"I play to win, mister. Everything is allowed."

He nodded once, stood and slid his briefs down his long legs, and she sat, frozen, transfixed by the sight of his erection, thick, jutting and completely involved. "We still have tiles," she muttered, not wanting to play anymore. Right now, she had places to go and large cocks to sit on.

Being the world's most clueless man, he smiled. "Then we play on."

He made a great show of playing with his pieces, and stealthily, Jenn's fingers crept between her thighs, settling there, and oops, her finger accidentally inserted itself inside her. He looked at her oddly, but played out his letters.

E-N-T-E-R.

"And what am I supposed to do now?"

"Play on," he said, and frustrated, she used her free hand and shifted her tiles. However, before she could lay them out, he laid his hand over hers.

"Not the tiles," he told her, and then she understood.

Oh, my.

"Move your chair," he instructed, and she swallowed at the thought. However, Jennifer considered herself a good sport, so she scooted her chair out from under the table in plain view.

"Play on," he repeated in a husky voice, his gaze focused firmly on her hand.

At first she felt awkward and nervous and not inclined to trip the light fantastic, but he was quiet and still, making her feel almost as if she was alone. Or at least that's what she told herself.

She parted her legs, displaying herself more than she'd ever done before, and her fingers began to move. Steadily she stroked, blocking out the sight of him until the pleasure began to take over, and then she lifted her eyes, locked with his, and her fingers began to move in earnest.

He was a courteous audience, only a slight hitch to his

breathing, a line of sweat on his brow, and she could feel her body moving to climax. Faster she stroked, chasing the orgasm, feeling it flutter inside her as warm and damp as the summer's air.

He didn't make a move to touch her, didn't try to interfere, and her hips began to rise and fall, wanting to chase the flutters, wanting to come.

Eventually she could feel the shudder of the climax, and she closed her eyes, letting her fingers do magic, her hips tilting as high as they could.

There. There. There.

For a moment, she stayed there, frozen, aftershocks of nerves pulsing between her thighs, and she opened her eyes, met his, and forgot to breathe.

She had never seen a man so pained, so primed, and yet he sat there, frozen, locked inside himself. She wanted to go to him, wanted to climb into his arms, and if he had said a word, she would have, but he didn't, and so she shifted back in her chair, not as sated as she would like, and she blamed it all on him.

Defiantly she lifted her hand, took her well-worked finger and slipped it between her lips.

A sound emerged from his throat, low and raw. But still he didn't speak.

She studied her letters, and then laid out her word.

E-M-B-R-A-C-E.

Blandly she met his eyes, and he looked her, appearing lost and uncertain, and she could feel her heart twist.

"What do you want from me?" he asked, and this time, because he asked, she went to him and straddled him, lowering herself over his cock.

"This," she said, taking his lips, kissing him and showing him her heart. His mouth was hungry and angry and hard. She wanted to go slow, she wanted to be tender, to show him how to love, but he was past that, and he lifted her on the table, pulled her legs around him, and began to piston inside her, using her for purposes that she couldn't understand.

Later, after her thighs were raw, after her back was bruised, after her heart had been raked over the coals, he emptied himself inside of her, and pulled her upright, soothing her back, stroking her hair, but the burnt embers on her heart remained.

IT WAS LATE ON Tuesday morning, and Jennifer was snug in Aaron's bed, listening to the battle of the typewriter keys. He was careful about his work, never sharing too much, hoarding his privacy, but sometimes she would pretend to be asleep, just so that she could watch the way he worked.

Before dawn, when the sunlight was absent, he worked by the light of an antique gas lantern. He'd told her that the warmer light was better for the eyes, but she didn't believe it. Sometimes he would sit in the dark, staring into that flickering flame, and it was clear that more than his work was occupying his mind.

He chewed gum when he worked. Anxious, loud popping, his jaws working furiously. In between these bouts of inspiration, he would pull at his hair in what had to be a painful manner. Sometimes he would hunch over the keys, his fingers flying as he typed. Other times he would stare at the typewriter with a ghostly gaze that looked beyond the machine, beyond the cabin, and she wondered where he went. Where were the places he wanted to go?

Whenever he was unhappy with his words, Aaron would rip the paper from the roller, muttering to himself. "Hack," "Overdone," or her favorite, "You unimaginative cretin."

Although she was dying to see what he wrote, she never

asked. Out of all the pieces that Aaron kept tucked away, his writing was the one thing that he nurtured most of all, and she knew it.

This particular morning, he was in the midst of a flurry of pages, muttering unhappily when Jenn heard the knock at the door.

Aaron raised his head, glared at the offensive sound, and Jenn snatched up her clothes.

"Who is it?" he asked in a voice that would have scared off little puppies, small children or dedicated delivery men.

A heavily accented voice came from the other side of the door. "Do you have so many guests in this dreadful hellhole? Do not insult me with stupid questions."

Jenn was surprised to see him smile, and he turned to look at her.

"You're decent?" he asked, and she threw on a T-shirt and jeans.

"Not really, but you can open the door anyway."

A minute later, a tiny old woman swept into the room, tossing a black silk shawl over her shoulders, and nearly whacking Aaron in the face with her fringe. "I abhor nature. Why must you subject me to this…" Her unimpressed gaze found Jennifer and stayed there, accompanied by a profound silence that would have bothered a lesser woman. As it was, Jenn was perhaps intimidated, but she managed a brave front.

"I'm assuming you are not the housekeeper," the woman stated.

Jenn looked at Aaron, and realized this was a test. He wanted to see if she would crack under pressure. Ha. No wimps here. Undaunted, she crossed her arms across her chest. "Not the housekeeper."

"Nor the plumber," the woman continued, tapping one finger on her chin.

"No."

"Nor the personal trainer who is here to help Aaron achieve the washboard abs he's always craved?"

Jennifer looked at Aaron and arched her brow. "Seriously?"

Aaron began to smile. "Didi, this is Jennifer Dade. Jennifer, this is Didi Ziegler. My agent."

"And who is she to you?" asked Didi, not happy with a mere name. Jenn suspected she wanted the complete Jennifer Dade dossier, short as it was.

"That's complicated," answered Aaron, and Jennifer smiled at him gratefully.

"I suspect it's much simpler than that, but we shall pretend to be polite and ignore it. I am here to check on your progress, as I have promised, only to have my meager hopes dashed each time I appear. So tell me, Aaron, do you have something for me? Something to make me weep with joy, soften the pains and frustrations of being your agent. If you want to please me, say yes."

"Not yet."

Didi directed a pointed scowl at Jennifer, obviously considering her responsible for sloth, gluttony, lust and a host of other sins, except envy, which Jenn knew was impossible. One foot began to tap disapprovingly on the floor, and not that Jenn wanted to read bad things into it, but the message was there.

It was completely unfair because Jennifer knew that Aaron was working, knew that every day he was seated at his typewriter, with a discipline that few could ever match. She opened her mouth to say something when Aaron interrupted.

"That's not why," he said, which could be construed

to mean that he was defending her. But why not simply give his agent something to read? It was the easier route. Puzzled, Jenn watched him, noted the stubborn edge to his jaw. A mystery was afoot.

Didi kicked at the paper balls on the floor, and Two hissed from his perch on the bookshelves. "Do you think I will wait forever?" she asked.

"Yes," he answered simply, a man used to taking women for granted. There was a message there; Jenn chose to ignore it.

Jenn thought that Didi would have been disappointed. Heck, she would have been. Heck, she would have fired him. But instead Didi patted Aaron's cheek, and gave him a warm smile. "Forever is much longer than you believe." Then she considered Jennifer, taking in the mussed hair, the lack of makeup and the faint rose of sunburn on her arms. "I don't know you. I probably will not like you, but I find myself full of questions."

"She's a reporter."

Didi's mouth gaped, only slightly, only for a second, but Jenn noticed. Then Didi closed it, and wheeled to face Aaron. "You are a stupid, stupid man."

"I know," he said, and again the older woman paused.

Seeing her silence, Aaron smiled at Didi, a full smile without pain or effort. There was an odd relationship to them, a crusty familiarity, and Jenn believed that yes, the word was commonly called *affection*.

Curiously the woman watched him, then gave one dismissive nod before heading for the door, her heels tapping with brisk efficiency. "Very well. I will leave now, and after I leave, will you forget me? Forget your obligation? Forget the woman whose very livelihood depends on you?"

"Forget you? Never. Believe me, I've tried."

Didi laughed, a surprisingly loud laugh for such a small woman. "Very good. I will try to keep the disturbing ramifications of this inglorious tryst out of my brain, but I will be back."

AFTER DIDI HAD LEFT, Jennifer started to laugh, and Aaron liked to listen to her laugh. He hadn't realized the sounds that he missed before Jennifer. Laughter. She liked to laugh, and liked to smile, and he realized that he liked it, too. Watching her laugh and watching her smile.

"That's your agent? She's delightful."

"I'm glad you have a sense of humor."

"How long have you two worked together?" she asked, and he could see the questions in her eyes. The ones she asked, and the ones left unsaid.

"Fifteen years."

"How old are you?"

"Thirty-four," he answered, and she looked at him, surprised. "You thought I was older?"

"Yes," she told him, decimating his ego. "You must have been some prodigy? Either you're very good, or she's very stupid."

"She lived with my father when I was a kid. It was short. It ended badly, but somehow in the process, she developed a strong interest in my writing, and I gained an agent. I think she felt sorry for me."

"That would explain it."

Yes, he thought that it would, relieved to see the speculative light disappear from her eyes. Sometimes she got too close, and he wasn't sure he wanted to lie to her anymore. But there was a guilt-induced confessional, and then there was full, voluntary disclosure of exactly who he was, and how much of a bastard he could be.

Aaron didn't want her to know that.

There were parts of Aaron Barksdale that Jennifer would understand, but there were also parts of Aaron Barksdale that she wouldn't forgive. When she looked at him, those all-seeing eyes boring through his jerry-rigged facade, he regretted that he didn't say more. But it wasn't enough to make him return to the city and fix all those little missteps that he'd taken in his life.

It would have been a lot easier if one of those little missteps wasn't his son.

THEY SETTLED INTO AN odd sort of routine. Every morning, Jenn would go into town, and interview the seventy-year-old schoolteacher who had once taught FDR's granddaughter, do a taste testing for the double-chocolate-chunk cookies that had once been third runner-up in the Pillsbury Bake-Off and meet with a few other locals for an update on how the Festival's arrangements were progressing.

One afternoon she discovered Aaron's afternoon trips to read the paper, and spent the next half hour debating the implicit unbiased nature of the paper. She believed the *Times* was completely neutral, but Aaron told her that she needed to stop being so blind. Eventually he felt guilty and bought her a hot fudge sundae, and she let him solve the crossroad puzzle, only butting in to tell him that the answer to ten across was *Watergate*.

She wrote late into the afternoon, and then meet Aaron for dinner at his cabin. Sometimes they would stay there, make love, and sometimes she would drag him out to her rock, where she tried to educate him on the wonders of mobile communication. Aaron chose to remain ignorant.

Every day he told her more about the summers at Harmony Springs, but every day, he volunteered less and less about Aaron the man. She did discover a few pertinent facts: he possessed no driver's license because a man's feet were transportation enough. He had lost his virginity at age fourteen to a senior in high school, HS 147, which told her he had one time lived in Brooklyn. He had never gone to college because he believed that the institution of secondary education was flawed when compared to life experiences. Jennifer, who had graduated—barely—from NYU, scoffed and told him that the only man who had matched Aaron's life experiences was John the Baptist and Albert Einstein. He laughed.

Sometimes at night they would stay awake, the room dark except for the single gas flame, and she would dare ask the questions that she never asked during the day.

"Don't you have dreams?" she asked, curled up against him, listening to the quiet sounds of the night. "Don't you want to be published again, or achieve...I don't know, something?"

"I'm here. All I want is to be. Everyone wants to make something of themselves, but they get caught up in making themselves into someone they aren't."

"Do you think I'm doing that?"

"No," he told her, punctuating his answer with a kiss on her hair.

"Don't you want anything more than this? You don't want money or fame or recognition or happiness or love?" Perhaps there was a subliminal suggestion in that last one, but he didn't seem to notice.

"Money isn't anything. You can have security and be poor. Fame is for the man whose ego needs inflating. Recognition? If I recognize what I am, if Didi recognizes what I am, what does it matter if a French nutter in bow tie and spectacles writes that I'm talented?"

She rose up on his chest and frowned. "It's vindication."

"Vindication is for people who don't believe in themselves."

With a frustrated sigh, she rolled back into the pillows. "What about happiness or love?"

"I'm happy."

She shot him her darkest look. "This is happy? Here?"

"Do you think I'd be happier in the city?"

"I think you'd be happier around people," she stated firmly.

He stayed stubbornly silent, not agreeing with or denying her statement.

She rolled on top of him, feeling his heart, feeling his cock, and knowing he wasn't nearly as unmoved as he pretended. "Don't you miss the world? Don't you miss conversation? Don't you miss laughing?"

"I make myself laugh. You make me laugh."

"Don't you miss being touched?" she asked, kissing his neck.

"You're here."

"I won't always be here," she reminded him.

"No. You won't," he agreed, and his voice was terribly flat.

"Won't you miss me? Won't you miss this?"

"Yes."

"But not enough to leave this place, not enough to leave your tower?"

"No."

"I'm going home."

He sat upright, and for once, his voice was not so flat. "To New York?" he asked, panicked. Slightly. It wasn't enough.

Jenn picked up her clothes, because every night she gave him a little more of her heart, and every night his heart stayed unmoved. Tonight she had no more heart left to give. "I'm going home to my cabin. If you need me, you'll know where to look. It's not that far."

By the time the sun rose, her tears were dry, her mind was clear, but her heart still wasn't her own.

THERE WERE TIMES WHEN Aaron knew he was a difficult person. He had lived his life with difficult people, and it wasn't until he was midway through his twenties that he realized that difficult people weren't the norm. According to his calculations, which he knew were accurate, Jennifer had exactly three days left in Harmony Springs.

He knew he should have said something to her last night, but for the first time in his life, he had no words. He hunched over his typewriter, trying to battle his way through the scene, but his fingers felt clumsy, and he ended up staring into space.

What was she doing? Was she in town, had she packed up and left? That thought chilled him so much that he stopped frowning at the blank page, and pulled on his shoes and stalked down to her cabin.

There, tucked safely in her bed, was Goldilocks. Her clothes were thrown over her chair, her phone was vibrating, and there were tear stains on her cheeks.

Bastard.

Aaron nearly backed away, because he knew he would never go to the city, he knew what Jennifer wanted and he knew that he couldn't give her that. He didn't want her world, he didn't want her life. All he wanted was her, and it was a treacherous need inside him. An emotional need that terrified him because he had needed his father, he had needed the soft burn of alcohol, and both had ripped up his soul.

But Jennifer wouldn't do that, he protested to himself.

No, he couldn't give her everything that she wanted, but he could give her some peace, and not bothering to undress, he climbed under the sheet, and pulled her into his arms. She breathed out a sigh, and curved into him, as if she belonged. Work forgotten, he stayed with her, holding her close, letting her sleep.

The sex was the easy part. It was the humanity that damned him.

THERE WAS A STOPWATCH on her phone. A little timer that flashed in the corner showed Jennifer exactly how many hours she had remaining. She didn't like to look at it because when she did, a great ache rolled in her stomach.

That night, Aaron was slaving over the typewriter, not exactly writing, but making a good show of it, and Jennifer chose to pretend that it didn't matter. To make it clear that he didn't matter, she put in her headphones and stared at the display on her phone, noticing with satisfaction the way he kept turning around and looking at her, and then returning to his work.

Eventually he came to bed and sat down beside her, looking at her phone.

"What are you doing?" he asked, and she pointed at her earbuds.

Apparently unhappy with her answer, he jerked them out of her ears.

"What?" she said with a scowl.

"What are you doing?"

"Watching a movie."

He looked at the tiny display, and squinted. "That's a phone. You use a television to watch a movie, or a theater screen."

And yes, perhaps her arms gestured a tad overdramatically. "Do I see a television screen here? No. Do I see a theater screen here? Nay. I am forced to improvise, hero-ically retrofitting whatever is at my disposal. Namely the phone."

And yes, perhaps he sensed that Jennifer was in a pissy mood, but did he choose a topic that was designed to ease her out of her pissiness?

"What are you watching?" he asked, choosing instead to talk about her phone.

It was tempting to put the headphones back in her ears. She refused. *"Princess Bride."*

"Mawkish pabulum."

"How long have you been waiting to spit that one out? I'll have you know that before *Princess Bride* was a movie, it was a book. A great book."

"It was all right. They really made a movie?" he asked, now choosing to talk about crass commercialization of media entertainment, and she knew in her heart that this was a peace offering. A more ambitious woman would have demanded more.

"Oh, you are such a greenhorn," Jennifer muttered, try-ing to sound like the more ambitious woman she wasn't. Instead it came out like a moonstruck declaration of love, which perhaps it might have been.

He smiled and sat down next to her on the bed, and because it was a night for miracles, he started watching.

"The dialogue isn't that good," he commented, a token critique designed to show his disdain for crass commercial-ization and the lemmings who were a slave to it. Sometimes he was far too transparent.

She shot him a sideways look that said she wasn't buying it. "It's meant to be satirical. Yet still have heart. You might have trouble with that concept. Mawkish. Pabulumish."

"You don't need to make fun."

"I have learned from the master."

"Did I teach you that?"

"No, my seventh grade English teacher did, but I picked up some great pointers from you. Shh. This is the good part."

THE DAY BEFORE SHE was scheduled to leave, Jenn had most of her story written. Nothing earth-shattering, but it was respectable and fun. It was the history of Harmony Springs. The people, the stories, the lives that this town had touched.

It wasn't hard to write about because she hadn't escaped unscathed, either. It wasn't the cute little town that had touched her. Not its colorful characters or the cheerful music or the small-town charm. No, it was Aaron.

She didn't want to name what was between them. It was ironic to think that she'd finally found the one man who she wanted to be with, and sure, he loved having sex with her, he loved talking to her, he gave her thoughtful little presents and displayed an odd sort of desire. But in the end, when she left this place, he was going to say goodbye and that'd be all.

The End.

She wanted to scream. She wanted to hit him. She wanted to kiss him and love him and ride him until he begged for mercy. These emotional wrestling matches were only eased with a daily trip to Frank's for ice cream, or a nightly lovemaking session with Aaron. Sometimes both.

It was early on her last morning, and she was in that half-awake time found somewhere after sex and after dreams, but before caffeine could shock her awake. She rubbed her palms over her face. As always, he was in his chair, far far away, but he was watching her with his writer's eyes.

"My name is Aaron Barksdale."

It took a second for the name to register, and Jenn sucked in a breath.

And she called herself a journalist?

Yes, she'd imagined a lot, but she'd never imagined that. The Booker Prize, the Pulitzer, a literary wunderkind at the young age of twenty-two. Authors like Aaron Barksdale didn't hide away in the woods. They went to book parties, they dined with their agents, and they didn't fall in love with ordinary people like her.

"Why didn't you tell me?" she asked him, sounding surprisingly calm and composed. Maybe she'd learned that from him. Maybe she'd learned how to brick that wall inside herself, slowly suffocating the cask of her heart.

"It's not something I tell people," he explained, which was, frankly, a stupid explanation. He'd danced with her, he'd had sex with her, he'd shown her his work. He should have trusted her.

And now he was trusting her? Right as she was about to leave? Oh, yeah, so why didn't she believe that? "Why are you telling me now?"

"It's a test."

Oh, goody. Jenn hated tests. "What sort of test?"

"You're a reporter. You need a story. I just gave you a story. So, are you going to use it?"

Slowly her blood began to simmer, to stew and finally, to boil. Oh, he was so clever. So sure of her. So absolutely positive that she was going to stab him in the back. As if she could. "If I write this up, you'll never forgive me, will you? If I don't write this up, I lose my job. You think I'll write it, don't you?"

His nod was instant. The bastard didn't even have to think about his answer. "Your job is important. This is your chance."

"And you want me to write about you? You want me to expose your dirty little secret?"

"Technically there is no dirty little secret."

"Do you want me to write the story, Aaron?" she repeated, tired of trying to guess the right answer.

"No." His face was so clinical, so cold. She rubbed her arms in spite of the warm summer air.

"So what's the test?"

He stayed silent, waiting for her to figure it out, waiting for her to comprehend the crooked complexities of his mind. And eventually she did. Because she'd learned that from him, as well.

"You think I will, don't you? You think, oh, yeah, she's going to screw me over. You're longing for me to screw you over on this one because then you'll be right. All your little distrusting obsessions with people. Everybody is out to get you, and oh, look. There's No-Ethics Jennifer, she was out to get me, too. And if I write it, then you'd be right."

She stalked around the room, but he didn't move, didn't flinch. "Is it worth that much to you to be right, Aaron? Is it worth giving up all this little sanctuary that you've built just to know that humanity is always in it for the bad?"

"Does that mean you're going to write the article?"

He looked so sure of himself, so sure of her. His mind had mapped this all out because he wanted to hate her. Oh, he needed to hate her. God forbid the man should actually care.

Jenn picked up the nearest object, conveniently a dictionary, and chucked it in his direction. He dodged it easily, not angry, not afraid, as immovable as stone, which only infuriated her more.

She wasn't a thrower. She wasn't a violent person. She wasn't a screamer. And most important of all, she wasn't a woman who stabbed the man she loved in the back.

"Screw you, Aaron. Screw you and your Pulitzer. Screw you and your artistic temperament."

"You're mad."

"Yes, I'm mad."

"Why?" he asked, steepling his fingers, watching her as if she was a stranger.

To prove her anger, she threw another book at him, and even Two moved out of her way. The cat knew human nature much better than the man. "What is this?" she raged. "Fodder for the book, Aaron? Playing the puppet master, pulling the strings. Plunging the depths of the human condition to see how far they will sink?"

"No."

She stared at him, with his cool blue eyes and his granite heart and his talented hands.

No. He wasn't worth it. He wasn't worth this pain, but the pain wouldn't leave, so she would.

"I'm going back to the city. I'm going home. To men who don't treat me like a lab rat. To a place where I can have showers and towels and walk four blocks to four different coffee shops, and men will whistle when I walk by. Because there is nothing for me here. Nothing? Do you understand? You are nothing to me. Goodbye."

With a great show of force, she slammed the door behind her, hoping she'd disturbed him, hoping she'd unsettled his omnipotent existence. Hoping she'd hurt him as brutally as he'd just gutted her.

9

THE FIRST NIGHT she was gone, Aaron wrote himself into a frenzy. Pages and pages of rambling tripe that was hokey and contrived. He was trying for the best sort of Joyce, a meandering stream of consciousness to fully show confusion and frustration, but ended up with the bad merging of a schoolgirl's diary and *Penthouse Letters*. He told himself that he was better off without her, better without the distraction, but then he wrote the words *surging passion* and nearly slit his wrists.

His father would have laughed. His father would have been right to laugh at him.

By the time the sun rose, the lantern had flickered down to the stub of a wick, and the wooden floor had disappeared beneath the mounds of garbage that he'd written the night before.

Two was having a field day, flicking the pages with his paw and staring up at Aaron with his you-poor-ignorant-human look that in the past had made Aaron smile.

Now he thought the stupid cat was right.

He should never have told Jenn the truth. He shouldn't have dangled the bait. He should have stayed silent, said goodbye and went on as before. As soon as Frank's was

open, he walked over and bought a copy of the paper, ob-
sessively checking each page, because he knew he was
right.

Of course she'd write the story—it was too good. Her
job was on the line. Why, in his own perverse way, he'd
saved her job for her. She would be grateful.

He'd double-checked each page twice, but didn't see
anything, and decided that Jenn would do fact-checking
first. She'd do research. Hell, she'd probably interview his
father. That thought brought a tight smile to his face. Too
bad he was going to miss that one. Being thorough, she'd
dig through all the rumors and all the innuendo and find
the ugly truth. No, there would be nothing in print until
she'd held up his life for the public's consumption.

The next day he checked and the day after. And the day
after that. And every night his floor disappeared under the
great mounds of meaningless words.

For nothing.

It was two weeks before he realized that she wasn't
going to write the article about him. And why not? It was
a lot edgier than the stories about Lillian's literary salons.
A bunch of misdirected elitists who sat around, spinning
their tales and sharpening the blade of their wit and not
giving a damn about who got in the way.

"Where is the girl?" Didi asked.

"She went back to the city."

"I see."

"No you don't."

"Did you chase her off?"

"No. It was an assignment. Two weeks. The end."

"Sounds very predictable. You look more fatigued than
usual. I'm assuming you're not sleeping, judging by the
great moons under your eyes."

"Leave it alone, Didi."

"Would you, Aaron? Would you leave me alone if I was in pain?"

"No," he admitted, hating that she was right.

"Do not be more stupid than you must."

"She knows who I am."

"She figured it out? Very clever."

"I told her," he admitted, not very clever.

Behind the giant lenses, her eyes saw more than he wanted. "I could have predicted it. She has that eager lap-dog way that encourages such foolish things."

"She was supposed to write an article."

"An article? About you? Imagine. I would expect my phone to be buzzing, people asking about your return from the dead, but *mein Gott,* it has been silent. What would that mean, I wonder? Is there no article or are you not news? Which would be worse?"

From above him, Two hissed in male solidarity.

"You are stewing. Do not stew. Go talk to the girl. Squander the remainder of your self-respect and give her flowers and jewelry and write odes to her hair. She will enjoy that, it's very *People* magazine."

"She writes for the *Times.* Or she did. I don't think she'll talk to me."

Didi smelled the blood in the water, and her smile grew wide. "It must have been a nasty fight. I would have loved to have been a fly on the wall. I need the excitement, although it's probably bad on the heart."

"I can't do this, Didi."

She muttered something foreign and rude. "What? Be human? Sometimes when you try very hard, you manage a passable imitation. It is regrettable, but you are so much softer than you want to be. Don't be your father, Aaron. He isn't worth it. He wanted to believe he was God, but you were the only one who ever bought into his myth. You will surprise yourself with what you can do. Go."

Didi had always believed in the fiction he wrote, and was a little more tenderhearted than she wanted to appear, but today he needed to hear this. He needed to believe in his fiction, as well. "I could hug you."

"Please restrain these wild impulses. You would muss the hair and ruin my professional disposition. I must leave before this turns sentimental and mawkish."

The door slammed with excessive force, but as she walked down the path, there was a spry kick in her step. A momentary recognition of the impossible achieved. However, the movement was so slight that only an astute observer of human nature could notice.

Aaron didn't notice it at all.

THE WEEK FROM HELL continued when the pink slip came, swift and impersonal, in the form of an e-mail. Not that Jenn was surprised, and she actually enjoyed Quinn the Sleazebag's positive comments on her performance and his assurances that he would be happy to provide her with a letter of recommendation. He sounded almost sincere. Not that her performance could ever match Lizette's.

Jenn felt the haze of cynicism momentarily cloud her normally rosy-eyed vision. Yeah, if only she'd gotten a little drunker at the office holiday party, then the ending might have been different. Of if she'd written about Aaron, sure, she'd be the office hero. It was a sad day in Mudville when a reporter needed a slimeball bag of tricks to get ahead. It almost made her reconsider her ethical high-ground position. Almost.

Of course, if Jenn didn't like the taste of ramen noodles and peanut butter, she might have been a little less firm.

The plus side of unemployment was that the bad foods she craved were also the cheapest.

Sorry, Mom. Gotta eat Twinkies because broccoli costs too much.

It was easy to joke and smile because if she didn't, she'd spend all her days in tears.

She still couldn't believe that Aaron had expected her to write about him, expected her to cheapen everything they shared; that was a gazillion times more painful than layoffs. That insult almost made her forget about him, forget about the time together, forget about the nights on the rock, forget about the nights in his arms.

Who was she kidding?

After she had packed up her desk, her diploma and her favorite coffee mug, her roommate took her out for dinner. Natalie was paying, but the day didn't get any brighter. There were some roommates that were like ghosts. Impersonal, nonintrusive and understanding of the basic Roommate Code of Conduct: We Don't Have to Be Friends. Unfortunately Natalie was one of those special people who thought she was friends with everyone, and as such could speak with absolute candor and honesty and a beauty-pageant smile.

The restaurant was a favorite of Jenn's, heavy on dessert. A little out of her price range, but tonight, that was Natalie's problem, not Jenn's. It actually felt nice to unload some of her burden on her roommate with her six-figure income and her banker boyfriend. Jenn's mother loved Natalie. 'Nuff said.

"Look, I don't mean to be harsh or anything," Natalie started as soon as the menus were down. "I know you've got a lot on your mind, but is this going to cause a problem with the rent?"

Jenn wavered between the cheesecake and the

cheeseburger, thinking the cheeseburger had more nutrients, but the cheesecake would make her happy. Happy was good. Jenn liked happy. She put down the menu and met Natalie's eyes with confidence that no sane woman would ever feel. "It won't be a problem. I had some interviews yesterday. I can work two, maybe three jobs at minimum wage. We'll be fine."

Sarcasm was routinely lost on Natalie, and she nodded with relief. "Good to hear it. What are you thinking? The cobb salad looks good."

Jenn glanced down the entrées and reaffirmed her commitment to culinary happiness. Vegetables be damned. "I'm thinking the cheesecake and a glass of pinot grigio."

Natalie leaned in close in that confidential I'm-your-therapist sort of way. "You know, this is a great teachable moment for you. Whenever bad things happen to me, I always binge. Mallomars are my drug of choice. And the next day, I look at the mirror and see that little pooch in my tummy and I tell myself it isn't worth it. Do you really want to look in the mirror tomorrow and have the thousand-calorie regrets? Just saying."

When the waiter appeared, Jenn ordered first, choosing to be firm and decisive. "I'll take a cheeseburger, the cheesecake, and keep the pinot coming." After he left, she looked at Natalie and shrugged. "I wish I had your will-power, Natalie, I really do. Maybe someday I'll be strong. I can only hope."

And somewhere in hell, the devil and Jenn were dining on their cheesecake, and giggling might have been involved. Just saying.

IT WAS THREE WEEKS later when the first peace offering arrived. A bag of coffee from Guatemala. Buried deep within the beans was a typewritten note that she didn't discover until she poured them into an airtight container.

"From Coban. They're light, slightly acidic, and can leave a bitter aftertaste if not brewed properly. I knew you'd enjoy them."

She didn't want to smile. She didn't want to admit that she could be swayed with such cheap tactics like coffee bribery. She was.

The next box was a tin of beans from Yemen. And did he say, "I'm sorry. I shouldn't have thought that you were capable of such black-hearted villainy, even if it meant your job"? Oh, no. Instead, she got little messages like: Earthy and complex. Handpicked under fair-trade standards. Dean and Deluca say it's the best.

Any other woman would have been dancing a jig to be freed from the clutches of a Pulitzer Prize–winning writer who didn't know beans about emotional connections. Not Jenn.

She was no other woman, and she was defending her position on that very subject over a pitcher of margaritas with Martina.

"I hate him."

"Yes, I can see the hate oozing from your pores. Oh, no. That must be the tequila."

"What am I supposed to do?"

"Whatever you do, don't call him."

"I don't think he has a phone."

"That's very convenient. If you get really desperate and want to go see him, you'd have to actually take a ninety-minute train ride to humiliate yourself. It's like a reinforced sanity check. Not all women are so lucky." She noticed Jenn's sheepish expression. "I'm assuming that you talked yourself out of it."

"It was peak train fares, and I can't afford to pay for it. Off-peak, I'd spring for it, but he's not worth peak."

"No. None of them are. Have another margarita. You'll feel better until the hangover hits."

No, she wouldn't. A hangover was preferable to this misery. "Do you think he'll ever talk to me or see me, or will he continue to torment me with thoughtful gifts that rate zero on the Dr. Marian Dade scale of man-worthiness?"

"Eventually he'll be back for the sex. They always come back for the sex."

Jenn buried her head in her hands. She didn't want to think about sex, but here she was, drinking margaritas and thinking about sex. "It was good sex. I miss it. I miss him. He's worth a peak ticket."

"Be strong, Jenn."

"You know that my life would be much better if strong was my middle name."

"What is your middle name?"

Jenn lifted her glass, eyeing the frozen green concoction and its tangy rim of salt. "Tequila."

THERE WERE A LOT OF advantages to working at Starbucks. Good benefits, free coffee and a certain flexibility to her schedule. The days passed, and each morning there was a package of coffee at her door, but no phone calls, no visit, nothing to indicate that Jennifer was more to Aaron Barksdale than a coffee cup in need of filling.

There were other needs to be filled, and she might have been a little punchier, a little more stressed and sadly, a little poochier around the middle. Jenn really hated when Natalie was right.

It was a warm Tuesday morning when he came in her store. Jenn nearly poured coffee over the elderly gentleman who was probably a personal injury lawyer, but she stopped herself in time.

She wasn't sure if this was business or pleasure, so she opted for the worst.

"What can I get for you today, sir?"

Aaron looked tired and skinny and hurt, and perhaps it was cruel to be glad he was in pain, but Jenn had a low tolerance for sympathy these days, and Aaron wasn't getting any from her. Sympathy, that is.

"Why didn't you tell me?"

Upon first seeing her after six weeks, there were many things that he could have said. Things that would endear him to her. The assignment of blame, the wounded Bambi look and the anger in his voice were not the best choices.

Jenn flashed him her most nonendearing smile.

"We sell coffee here, sir, not personal therapy. What's it going to be? Frappachino or straight coffee. You don't look like a frou-frou frappachino type. I bet you're not."

He wasn't amused, stuffing his hands into his pockets. "When's your break?"

"Approximately fifteen years. Do you want to wait that long?"

He nodded once, taking the shot with grace. "How long are you going to be mad at me?"

"Approximately fifteen years. You want to wait that long?"

His eyes met hers squarely, never wavering once. "I would."

Oh, God. It was a low blow. Two succinct syllables precisely picked to deflate her anger and turn her into a quivering mass of hope and dreams and all those pesky things that made her mother worry.

Without further ado, Jenn looked at her watch, packed up her apron and announced to her coworkers she was going on break. "You have fifteen minutes," she instructed him as they headed out the door. He had fifteen minutes to make this right. Fifteen minutes to convince her that he was worth forty-two sleepless nights.

He didn't wait for privacy or common courtesy; instead he wheeled around as soon as they were around the corner, backing her up against the wall. "Why didn't you write the story?" She couldn't believe this. He acted as if he was mad at her, as if he was the victim.

She kicked her foot at the brick, hard, needing to destroy something, and her toe was all that was handy. "That really grates on you, doesn't it? You want so badly for me to write that slam job and destroy your life so you can stay hidden in the woods and feel sorry for yourself. I won't. Tell me what bothers you more. That I'm not a bottom-feeder, or that you'd have to admit that you're wrong?"

"I'm never wrong about people," he insisted, and she wondered why it was so important for him to assume the worst.

"You're always wrong about people. Get over it."

A delivery man yelled at Aaron, wanting him to move. Ha. As if. He glared at the man, who wisely went around.

Then he turned to Jenn, his mouth tightening into a hard line and his eyes turning to ice. "You like to make me hurt, don't you? Like to the take the knife and twist it, skewer me right in the heart."

Jenn jabbed a finger in his chest, right where his heart should be. That hollow cavity that now contained her heart, which made her all the more angry, especially when he grabbed her finger and held it like he didn't want to let go. "You don't have a heart," she insisted.

"I know."

He kept her hand, and the ice was gone from his eyes, the pain was back. "Why are you here?" she asked.

"To say I was sorry," he said, and then shut his mouth as if he was done.

Oh, no, not in this lifetime. The man used words for a living. He won the goddamned Pulitzer for those words. He could do better than that.

"You're here to say that Jenn is not a bottom-feeder, that she is a good person and cares enough about you not to hurt you. Isn't that right?" she prompted.

"Yes. All that."

"Are you going to let me keep putting words in your mouth?"

"Probably. I've missed you." He raised her hand to his lips, kissed it once, and she hated the way her knees went weak.

"You missed the sex," she said, needing to complain about something.

"Probably. When are you free?"

She wasn't going to be free of him ever again, but she wasn't going to tell him that. Not yet. He needed to earn his apology, and she wasn't done. "Seven," she said, pulling her hand away, retaining ownership of whatever body parts she could. Right now, the hand was the best she could do.

"We can go to dinner," he stated, his mouth twisted in that impassive way, and he seemed stubborn and certain and detached from the world. But the eyes gave him away. The eyes warmed her heart. "I want a chocolate soufflé for dessert," she demanded, needing to assert some level of control in this relationship, and dessert seemed a good place to start. "It's got to be the best in Manhattan."

"You can eat five."

She laughed then, breathing for the first time in weeks. "Will you ever tell me no?"

"No." Then he leaned over and kissed her, and it was better than chocolate, better than coffee, better than pride and self-respect. God, she loved him.

SHE HAD CHOCOLATE SOUFFLÉ from the Four Seasons. In bed. Jenn had never slept at the Seasons, although technically she hadn't done that yet either. Of course Aaron had rented a suite. The décor was everything that the campground at Harmony Springs was not. There were live flowers and mountains of pillows and wooden furniture that you found at Sothebys instead of Ikea.

And you'd think that when eating chocolate soufflé and staying in the most decadent room she'd ever seen, she would want to indulge in this fleeting moment of grandeur. You'd be wrong. All she wanted to indulge in was Aaron.

He lay back against the down pillows, looking uncomfortable and cranky. It didn't matter where he was, he never seemed to belong. His light blue eyes focused on her, and it touched her.

She'd missed him more than she had thought. Missed the scowling lines in his brow, missed the monosyllabic communications, and missed the feeling when he was moving inside her, and then, then…Jenn felt a sense of belonging that job security or chocolate could never bring.

The lights in the room were still blazing. She'd told him it was to admire the room. Actually, it was memorize him. She wanted to touch him and wanted to hold him, but he'd said so little to her and she had learned the hard way not to assume. So in absence of facts, the next best way to discover what she was dying to know was to interrogate.

She leaned over, regretfully moving the dessert. "What

finally did it? What finally got you into Manhattan? I mean, you could have delivered coffee forever."

"I couldn't kill you off anymore. I kept writing scenes. Love scenes. They weren't good ones, either."

"The work suffered?" she asked, sadistically pleased with the thought.

"I suffered. I kept thinking of you naked. My imagination wasn't enough."

"So what's it like to win the Pulitzer at twenty-three?"

"I don't remember. I was drunk. I spent a lot of time drunk."

"But you don't drink."

"Not anymore."

"Why did you quit?"

"I started drinking to fit the mold, to be more writerly. But at some point, it stopped being about the writing and more about the Scotch. That's when I stopped."

"Didi doesn't know you're still writing?"

"No."

"Why don't you tell her?"

Instead of answering, he looked at her plate. "Is that any good?"

She gave him a pass—for now—and took a bite of the dessert. "When are you going back?"

"In the morning."

"Will you come back?"

"If you'll let me," he said, as if she could deny him. The silly man still hadn't learned.

"You don't have to buy me any more coffee."

"You don't like gifts?"

"I love gifts. But I'd rather have you than the coffee,"

she told him, admitting the truth. He'd taken a large step toward her, and she wanted to respond in kind. It seemed only fair.

THE CLOCK BY THE BED said it was nearly four in the morning. Aaron thought she was sleeping, but he couldn't. His eyes wouldn't move from her, with her hand curled beneath her cheek, her breathing steady and sure. The night seemed shorter than he had thought it would be. He had convinced himself that one night of overindulging on her and the soul-destroying moment of being inside her would be enough to stop the dreams in his brain.

Diversions.

But a few short hours hadn't eased the frustration. His fingers were itching again, not to write, but because he wanted to touch her.

He missed her, and he hated to admit that moment of human frailty. Aaron didn't like being weak, didn't like putting something else first. He was a writer, a haunting shadow of a human being. He wasn't ordinary or simple, but she'd brought him lower than ordinary. She'd made him feel.

Feelings clouded his mind and made the world seem different.

As if she could feel the weight of his stare, her eyes flickered and opened, and although he should have felt guilty for waking her, he didn't.

"How's the job search?" he asked, racking his brain for some acceptable topic of conversation.

"Good. I have some leads. There's a weekly paper up in Westchester that will let me freelance, and I've written some articles on coffee—the world inside a coffee shop, the indignity of the coffee trade—and the effects of climate change on the cosmetics market."

"You're better than that," he said, worried because Jennifer should be reaching for more.

She looked at him, blinking the blur of sleep from her eyes. "I know, but thank you for saying it. I'll be okay. I'm tougher than I look, and now I'm poochier, too."

His hands moved over her, not writer's hands, but a lover's hands, but the compulsion to touch her was just as strong as his need to put down words on the page. Stronger. "I don't think you're very tough, and I don't see any pooch," he whispered, sliding down next to her, holding her, slipping a finger inside her. "Nothing here but a gentle softness and golden warmth. Nothing here but light."

She met his mouth and rode his finger, until his hands weren't enough. Silently he sank his cock inside here and she wrapped her arms around him. He had missed her, missed what she gave him. The world he lived in was a very dark place, but when she was surrounding him, all he could see was light. Golden, blissful light.

ROXANNE AND KEVIN KERSHNER lived in Queens, amidst a long line of row houses and tidy backyards, the very picture of New York suburbia. Before Aaron paid the cabbie, he nearly ran from the sameness of the neighborhood. For a man endlessly educated on the evils of a cookie-cutter world, the redundancy was stifling. Yet today he had something to prove. To himself. To Jennifer.

Roxanne answered the door, and he was surprised at how she'd changed. Nine years ago, she'd been a party girl with peroxide hair and spiked heels. Now she had soft brown hair and pink satin slippers with a penguin on the toe.

"Aaron?"

"Surprise," he managed awkwardly.

"Why are you here?"

"To see Kevin."

Immediately her eyes turned cold—not that he blamed her, but it only reinforced his cowardly belief that this had been a mistake. Pages could be rewritten, but not history. History, especially the bad sort, was for keeps.

"I don't think that's a good idea."

He nodded, choosing not to argue. "How is he?"

"Well."

"How are you?"

"Well."

"Good," he answered.

"You should go," she told him, and he almost left, but that wasn't what Jennifer would do. Jennifer would stay. She would barrel her way forward until she got exactly what she wanted. All he had to do was to think like Jennifer.

"I'd like to talk."

"We don't have anything to talk about."

"I want to know about him." It felt strange to think about his son, to wonder if the boy looked like Aaron, or if he had his father's imagination. Aaron had never allowed himself to venture that far into his own reality.

"It's a bad time," Roxanne explained with a quick, nervous smile.

Faced with Roxanne's smart-minded resistance, Jennifer would argue. Aaron could argue. "I don't think there's a good time, Roxanne. Don't make me go away. I won't have the courage to come back."

She stayed silent, hanging in the doorway, studying him, appraising his worth as father material. Eventually she nodded and let him in.

Their house was small and neat, filled with plastic toys and baseball gear and school pictures hanging in black plastic frames on the wall.

"You never married?" he asked, noticing the absence of another male.

"No. I gave up a lot with Kevin."

"I'm sorry," he apologized because he hadn't meant to wreck her life. Twenty-three-year-old men—twenty-three-year-old men with the literary world at their feet—were not supposed to be self-sacrificing. His mother had sacrificed her life for his father. His father had sacrificed Aaron for writing. And up until this moment, Aaron had sacrificed his son. Maybe it wasn't too late.

"Don't be sorry for my choices. I'm not." She pointed to the couch. Obediently Aaron sat, and she took the chair across from him.

"You grew up," he told her. The Roxanne Kershner he had known before spent as much time drinking as he had, and had hung on his every word.

"Have you?"

"I don't know. Can I see him?" He looked at the image of the boy on the wall, noticed the dark eyes, the studious glasses, the light hair that matched Roxanne's. There was nothing of Aaron in him, but that was probably a good thing.

"I told him about you."

"I assumed you would. Fathers aren't like Santa Claus. Their existence can't be rationalized away as a child gets older. How much did you tell him?"

"The truth. All of it."

"I suppose there was no reason to whitewash it."

"No." They stayed silent for a long time, and Aaron wanted to ask more. He wanted to know how many times the boy had mentioned him. He wanted to know if the boy hated his guts. He wanted to know thousands of details, things he had missed, but he didn't ask. Instead he folded his hands in his lap and assumed the same pose that he had assumed forever. Cool detachment. A man unmoved by life.

"You want to meet him?" Roxanne eventually asked, perhaps sensing that he wasn't going to move from her couch.

"I don't want him growing up thinking that I never cared enough to try." Aaron's father had never cared enough. Kevin Kershner didn't deserve that heritage.

"All right." Roxanne rubbed her palms on her jeans, and then left the room. Quiet voices leaked through the thin walls, and after an unsettling wait, mother and son returned. Roxanne hovered close to the boy, protective hands on his shoulders, as if Aaron could hurt him.

"Kevin. This is Aaron Barksdale," she introduced, as if Aaron was a stranger, because—of course—he was.

The boy stared at him, detached. Then he looked up at his mother, and asked, "Are we done?"

Aaron wasn't surprised. He knew the tone, the posture. The boy had a shell that was nearly as hard as his own. Aaron wasn't going to make this more difficult than it had to be, but he wanted him to know that the blame rested on Aaron's shoulders, not his.

"I wanted to see you. To know you."

"Too late," Kevin replied, his black eyes a fathomless pit.

"How is school?"

"We're out for the summer."

"Oh. Of course. Do you like it?"

"Science is okay. English sucks. I'm good at math. Mom says I get that from my father."

Surprised, he looked at Roxanne, noticed the way she ducked his eyes, and tucked the information away. "I hated science."

"Are we done?" his son asked, dismissing him.

Jennifer never let herself be dismissed, he reminded himself, and tried again. "I'd like to come see you again. I won't bother you or try to intrude on your life or try to make you my friend, but I would like to know you. And I'd like you to know me."

"Not interested. Are we done?"

Roxanne looked at Aaron. Aaron nodded, and the boy ran off, his departure punctuated nicely by the slamming of a door.

"Are you going to come back?" she asked.

"He hates me," Aaron stated, surprised by how much it stung. It was the ultimate human irony that the most expected response could hurt. If a man saw a knife aimed for his throat, he instinctively ducked. Yet if a man saw an icy shard of glass heading for his heart, he could only watch, wide-eyed and frozen. As a child, Aaron had picked many shards from his heart, and frankly he didn't like picking at them again.

"Are you going to come back?" Roxanne repeated.

"I'd like to, if it's all right with you." He met her eyes, and managed a poor imitation of a civilized smile. At first he thought she was going to refuse him, which would give him a fine excuse never to visit again. "Forbidden," he could tell Jennifer, accompanied by a helpless shrug. Of course then Jennifer would pester him until he dug in and tried again, beating his head against a brick wall while icy shards pierced his breast. If Aaron's sigh was long and heartfelt, it couldn't be helped. He was a man resigned to the pain of the human condition.

Frankly he'd rather be a zombie.

Roxanne glanced at the pictures, then looked at Aaron. "You don't have to. He's not your son."

A strange stillness settled over him, and Aaron told himself that he should be relieved, but it wasn't relief that he felt. Instead, it was as if someone had wiped his slate clean, erased the prior bad chapters of his life. Yet for some reason he was attached to that prior version. Or perhaps it was the idea of having someone that was his.

"You're sure?" he asked in an oddly disappointed voice.

"His father was a waiter at the hotel. It was either you or Mark, and you were the better choice. When he turned six, I knew. The eyes are his father's."

"Mark's good at math?"

"Yes."

Mentally Aaron picked another shard from his chest. He only wished Jennifer could appreciate it. "You have miserable taste in men," he complained.

"I know."

"Does he want a father?"

"Every boy wants a father," she stated, and it was true. Every boy wanted a father, a teacher to explain exactly how to be a man. Aaron was thirty-four years old, and he still wanted a father because he still didn't know how to be a man. However, he was learning.

"I can't pay you back," Roxanne added as if he cared about the money.

"You don't need to. You've already paid enough."

Nervously she glanced toward the back rooms where the boy who was no longer Aaron's son resided. "Will you ever tell him?"

"I don't know. He should know the truth at some point in his life."

"I know, but then he'll hate me. Right now, it's you he can't stand. If he's going to hate somebody, better you than me. I'm all he has."

She sounded worried about the possibility, but Aaron knew better, and he attempted to reassure her. "He won't ever hate you. You're his mother. You're his sun, his moon, his entire world. You can make all the mistakes in the world, and he won't stop loving you, won't stop needing you. A child is a very simple thing."

10

For the next week, Aaron spent the mornings riding the train into the city, and then haunting the various coffee shops of Manhattan. He didn't want to go to *her* coffee shop. He didn't want to disturb her work, but he needed to find a place to write because the cabin wasn't cutting it anymore. It felt too small, too isolated, and it made his skin itch like some metaphysical rash.

Unfortunately a typewriter was impractical for a commuter, so he used a Moleskin notebook and pen. He missed the visceral euphoria of crumpling up his pages and hurling them across the room, but he discovered a certain physical satisfaction when scribbling a particularly worthless paragraph into oblivion. While he was in the coffee shops, there was an energy and a solitude that he liked. He was a part of the world, and yet not. It reminded him of her, the buzz and hum, and he had discovered that with sound-reducing headphones, you never had to hear anyone talk at all.

He didn't tell Jennifer that he was making these commutes, although sometimes he picked her up after work, bought her dinner, and then took her back to his hotel where he could strip her naked and pour his body inside hers. Aaron told himself it was biology. Considering his lengthy isolation, an overactive libido was logical. Of course, he also created imaginary worlds where the sun had exploded, freezing all mankind, devolving the human species into something that more resembled an animal than man. Wisely Aaron chose not to delve further into the paradox of his own psyche.

He wasn't the only one. When they were together, Jennifer stopped asking her questions, which he thought was strange, but he wasn't one to complain—about *that,* at least. There were times when he suspected she was waiting on him to emote or communicate, neither of which were very likely, but they were working themselves into a companionable detente.

She called it a relationship.

The next night, he showed up at her apartment. "I know you're off tonight. I asked," he announced, quite proud of his detective work.

"You could have called and made arrangements. In advance." And of course, Jenn would always leap to the fast-track path, but Aaron liked his own, more pedantic pace, and besides, he had the perfect alibi.

"I don't have a phone."

"Come on, Aaron. How hard is it to buy a phone?"

"The coverage is really bad upstate. It'd be a waste." Phones were an unnecessary evil, chaining people to other people 24/7.

"You hate technology."

"There are links to cancer," he argued.

She leaned against the door frame and watched him with skeptical eyes. He didn't mind. "Oh, and now you become Mr. Current Events. When it's convenient."

There was a silent lull in the conversation, when she expected him to respond, but sometimes he couldn't. Sometimes he merely wanted to stare at her stupidly. In his writing, the protagonists didn't stare stupidly, or day-dream about wild sexual fantasies. Certainly they had sex, but it was a frenzied moment, usually designed to create complications rather than actually to bond. When he had sex with Jennifer, there was a bond. He didn't feel comfortable defining this bond, but it existed, and he knew that she felt it, too.

Which didn't explain why she never let him into her apartment. He held himself back from the entrance, where she hovered and guarded, and sometimes he worried that she was hiding some piece of her life from him. He frowned.

"What are you doing?" he asked, deliberately not peeping into her doorway like some voyeur. He crossed his arms across his chest to show her exactly how much he was not bothered.

"I'm giving you a hard time."

"Will I ever live this down?" he asked, hoping he never would. He liked it when she teased him.

"This isn't punishment. This is just my personality," she explained, and he thought that was acceptable, too.

"Okay, I can live with that." He waited for a beat longer before he knew she wasn't going to invite him in. And he hadn't come there for that. He had another purpose for tonight. "Come with me."

"Where?" she asked, going inside, grabbing the monstrosity she called a purse, and then she locked the door carefully behind her.

"I'll show you," he said.

The ball field was in Queens, a small park underneath the expressway, bounded by a bank building and a large highway sign with a sexy woman proclaiming that beer was good. There were two teams on the field—the Crushers and the Stingrays.

Aaron wasn't sure why organized sports couldn't be more creative. It was as if the sports gods had reached down with their thunderbolts and scribed a list of appropriately masculine animals, destructive weather anomalies and melodramatic verbs that sports writers adored. Like Crushers, for example.

He pulled the cap low on his head—not that he thought Kevin would recognize him...or acknowledge him, but he wasn't here to interact, only to observe. And to show Jennifer a small part of his life. Or actually, a small part that wasn't his life. He seemed to have a talent for that— collecting small pieces that weren't his.

"You like baseball?" she asked.

"He's my son."

"Which one?" She didn't look surprised, and he assumed she'd researched the rumors, but she'd never asked him. For that he was glad.

He nodded toward the north dugout. "The one on the bench. With glasses." Glasses were an unnecessary descriptor; Kevin was the only one on the bench.

"Are you going to speak to him?"

"No."

"Why?"

Of course now there were questions. Every time he opened the door, questions trampled inside with their muddy feet. It was the primary reason that Aaron believed in very rarely opening the door. But sometimes when Jenn didn't ask, and he wanted to tell her, the door was a little easier to open.

Kevin didn't seem to mind being alone. His chin was up, and his gaze was glued to the sky, looking somewhere beyond the game. His shoulders were thin.

"We're not at that stage of the relationship," was the best explanation Aaron could think up.

"There are no stages in fatherhood. It starts when he pops out of the womb. It ends when someone dies. That's it. You're his father."

"Not technically."

"All right. Biologically."

Aaron stared at the boy, who was so like him in so many ways. "Not technically," he corrected.

"There is no gray in paternity," she corrected, and he nearly smiled.

"I'm not his biological father. He thinks I am. I thought I was. But I'm not."

"Oh."

He waited for her questions, but she was waiting on him. Eventually the silence grew too loud to ignore.

"I paid Roxanne a lot of money because I didn't want to be a father." There were men in the world who should be fathers, and Aaron wasn't one of them. Neither was his father.

She looked at him with her serious eyes, and finally the question came. The one he was expecting. "So what are you going to do?"

"I don't know," he answered honestly. Secretly he had hoped that she would tell him what to do. Jennifer seemed to instinctively know these things. She seemed to know about people in ways that Aaron never could.

"What do you want to do?" she asked. Another question.

"I'd like to go away."

"Then why are you here?"

"I don't know. I feel rather useless." And empty. He moved closer to her. He didn't want to touch her because sometimes he was afraid that he couldn't stop, but when he was closer to her, he didn't feel quite so alone.

"Does he need a father?"

"Probably."

"Does he think you're an ass?"

"Definitely."

She looked at the boy, and then at Aaron, and then she glanced back at the boy. "It'd be very easy to walk away," she told him in a silky voice. It was what she called her conscience voice. She seemed to use it a lot. "The kid thinks you're an ass. You don't want a son. You paid for the very privilege of not being a father. It looks like he sucks at baseball anyway."

Jenn never liked her conscience voice. She complained about it constantly. Aaron didn't like it, either. But sometimes he needed to hear it.

But the boy drew his eyes like a magnet, sitting on the bench like an immovable rock.

"I always wanted to play baseball," he told her, and he'd never told anyone that.

"I bet you suck at baseball, too."

"I've never tried."

"Then maybe you should," she suggested.

"What if I suck at it?" he asked her, because Aaron considered himself something of a perfectionist, and he didn't like sucking at things.

"You probably will until you get the hang of it," she answered, which was absolutely no comfort. Eventually the team ran off the field, giving each other lots of high fives and hitting and wrestling, but Kevin sat there alone.

"My father sucked at fatherhood," he said, very softly, hoping she wouldn't hear.

"I know," she told him.

"I'm not very good at this," he said, not so quiet this time.

"I know that, too."

Kathleen O'Reilly   *173*

She laid a hand over his and she had good hands. Soft and gentle when necessary. Like now.

"I'm glad you're here," he told her, and she looked up at him smiling, and he knew he'd done something good.

"See? What did I tell you? Already you're getting the hang of it."

"What if he hates me?" It was easier to talk about this now. Talk about the possibility of making a mistake. A large mistake. With a little person who didn't need to have any more mistakes.

However, Jenn seemed to be more forgiving of mistakes then he was. "Parenting Rule Number One. Start with the bribes."

Bribes? Good God. He was supposed to delve into a nine-year-old mind? "I don't know what a kid would want."

"I have the perfect suggestion. An iPhone. Educational. The Holy Grail of communication, and trust me, mister, you can use all the help you can get. And best of all, you can text."

Her eyes were sneaky and sly, and he knew what this was about. She wanted him to get a phone, too. Being sucked into that whirling vortex where original thought and critical reasoning would cease to exist. "Oh, no. Do I look like a lemming? Give me some other ideas."

She laughed, and it was as soft and gentle as her hands, and then she wrapped her fingers in his, and he thought he was getting the hang of it after all.

IN A BOLD MOVE OF social exploration, Aaron took her out to a party on the Upper West Side. Jenn wasn't sure exactly why they were going, and she definitely wasn't sure what to expect. A week earlier she had asked him once about his friends who lived in the city. Mainly she was curious about the other side of the man. She knew the curmudgeonly hermit from Harmony Springs, but the author was still a virtual black hole.

It was two days after her question, when he announced they were going to a party. There was a certain rebellious quality to that pronouncement, as if he was proving to her that he had friends. Jenn tried to explain to him that she didn't actually expect to *meet* his friends, it was more a conversational sort of inquiry about the existence of said friends, but he insisted, and determined to be optimistic, Jenn took this new *entre* into his life as manna from intimacy heaven.

To show her support, she even bought a new dress for the occasion. A figure-hugging silver sheath that showed off her curves and made her legs look longer than they actually were. When he picked her up, the look in his eyes said that he approved.

Aaron, on the other hand, was dressed in a somber black suit, dark tie and spotless black shoes. Funeral attire, she thought, steeling herself for whatever dirge lay ahead.

"Where are we going?" she asked after they climbed into a taxi and were careening through traffic at a death-defying pace.

"My editor's apartment. He's having a party."

"Oh," she said, a noncommittal expression of Swiss-like neutrality because she wasn't sure if meeting his editor was a good thing or bad. There was a hard line to his jaw that didn't encourage happy assumptions.

"We don't have to do this."

"He's having the party for me," he answered.

"I suppose it would be rude to skip your own party."

"If you want to, we could," he offered.

"Do you want to go?"

"No."

"Then we should skip it," she answered and hammered on the glass, prepared to get the cabbie to drop them off somewhere safer. Aaron's hotel, for instance.

"I can do this," he stated firmly.

"I know that, which is why we don't have to do this," she told him, trying to be perky and encouraging and supportive and probably failing.

"You don't need to lie," he said, his stance stubborn in his his funeral-black suit, determined not to go gently into the night. As a woman, Jenn knew that men were biologically driven to fight these winless battles, and she also knew that she couldn't stop nature, so she leaned back and let the taxi drive them off into hell.

A few minutes later, they arrived at the apartment, which was decorated in that minimalistic style that belonged to that fashionable designer motif: "People Don't Actually Live Here." The main room was full of white unstained overstuffed couches, and a wall of smudge-free windows. Surprisingly there were no bookshelves—which didn't speak favorably on Martin's respect for the printed word.

Jenn kept her arm tucked in Aaron's as he led her around the crowded room, introducing her to authors and editors and telling her names she was going to promptly forget. Fascinatingly enough, he was not surly in this small group. He was sophisticated, charming, urbane, and Jenn remained quiet, observing the happy smiles and tinkling laughs. The warmth in the room was as minimalistic as the design, and as the minutes droned on, she scarfed a lonely glass of wine because she was feeling more and more adrift.

At least Didi was there, glittering in a bloodred cocktail dress that suited her. Spotting Jennifer, she made her way over. "You cannot show fear here, darling. Smile."

Jenn managed a toothpaste-selling smile, and Didi

laughed. "Yes, much better. Now you look as if you belong. I'm surprised he brought you."

"I always find that summer is the season for miracles."

At that, Didi quirked her brow, before glancing over at Aaron. "Yes, it does seem so. We should do lunch," Didi promised, and Jenn smiled bravely.

"I'd love to."

"Do not cower. It is not becoming. If you must be with a man of prestige, you must show the world exactly why he is with you."

"Like a trophy?" Jenn asked, possibly sarcastic.

"Is that what you are?"

"No," Jennifer answered with as much dignity as a non-trophy could manage.

Didi rapped her with her tiny beaded bag. "Good. I do not like trophies. They are cold and metallic and hollow."

"Why is he here?" she asked, hoping that the party meant that Aaron had finally given Didi his manuscripts. He hadn't said anything, but their relationship had only just progressed past sex and coffee-buying into the murky waters of preliminary dating.

When Didi smiled at her this time, there was something resembling warmth. "You do not know? He is here because of you. And please do not assume those haughty diva airs because I do not share the limelight, and you would only embarrass yourself if you tried."

"Not a problem," promised Jennifer, taking another long slug of wine.

As the night dragged onward, Jennifer tried to keep up, but this was not her element. This was some bizarre scene from a bad science-fiction movie, possibly involving space travel, dinosaurs and clones.

With subtitles.

It was nearly midnight when the surprise of the evening appeared. Cecil Barksdale, live, in person and slightly intoxicated.

Father and son stayed on opposite sides of the room like opponents in a ring, but Cecil was doing a better job of ignoring his son than Aaron was doing of ignoring his father.

"Would you like to leave now?" whispered Jenn nervously, hopefully.

Aaron tilted back his head and laughed, which did not bode well. "You're not having a good time?"

"Fabulous," she told him through gritted teeth, hoping to get a surly remark in return, but he pretended to miss the sarcasm and smiled at her, a trophy smile, and she knew it couldn't get any worse.

"Are you going to introduce me, Aaron?" It was his father, and things just got worse.

Aaron pulled her into the crook of his arm, affectionate and loving and all those things that she knew he despised. "Jenn, meet the man who inspired me. Cecil Barksdale, the world's greatest undiscovered talent. Dad, this is Jenn Dade."

Jenn. He called her Jenn. He never called her Jenn. The father was similar to the son. Tall, lean, with the same cool blue eyes. Right now, those cool eyes were looking her over with an alcoholic-induced leer. Peachy.

Cecil raised his martini glass and flashed Jennifer a smile. "Lovely to meet you. A man needs his muse, I suppose. Aaron lost his long ago."

"I'm assuming the martini is your muse of choice," she answered politely with a nod to his glass.

Cecil started to laugh, and Aaron's smile grew a little dimmer. At last.

"Actually, it's gin," Aaron corrected.

Cecil shook his head. "Actually you're both incorrect. Sex is so much more satisfying than alcohol. Although sometimes the morning after can get awkward. Hangovers are much more painless."

And do did one answer that? *Retreat.* "I'm getting chilled. I think I'll get my jacket and we can leave."

It wasn't polite—she didn't have a jacket, but she needed to get out of this place, leave this old man, and be alone with Aaron the Grouch. She missed him and she wanted him back.

When Aaron looked at her, he nodded once, and she knew he got the message. "Let me tell Martin goodbye. I'll meet you at the door."

She scurried to the back room to retrieve her sanity. Unfortunately—because it was a night for unfortunatelies—she had been followed by Aaron's dad, who apparently sensed a captive audience.

Gee.

"You must be very proud of your son," she said, pretending to be polite while pretending to search for a pretend jacket.

"Proud of him? For what?"

"For his accomplishments," she reminded him because he seemed to have forgotten them, or at least pretended to.

Cecil laughed then, and it wasn't nice. "Oh. Yes."

"So you wanted to be a writer as well?" she asked, not so nice, either, but her head was pounding and she didn't like the way he disrespected his son. No parent should treat their child like that.

"I am a writer," he said as arrogant as his son.

"I'm sorry. I wasn't familiar with your work."

He leaned against the wall, swaying slightly, and she

didn't bother to keep him upright. Cecil Barksdale would have to do that all on his own. Which, unfortunately, he did.

"You wouldn't be familiar with anything I've done. Women with your particular talents wouldn't understand."

"What talents?" she shot back, feeling something new. Anger. Not pretending anymore.

"Oh, my darling Barbara, you are such a refreshing ingenue. I can see why he brought you out of the bedroom. You're like a dollop of ice cream, without the cherry, of course."

"The name's Jennifer, bub," she said, making a beeline for the door. "I think I should be getting back to Aaron."

He stepped in front of her, blocking her way. "He was never as good as I was," he bragged, sliding his hand down her arm. "But you probably know that."

"I think I'm leaving," she said, sidestepping him, but he cornered her against a cold white dresser and planted a wet kiss on her mouth, right before he was forcibly removed.

And thrown against the wall by his only son.

"Are you okay?" Aaron asked her, his eyes calm and cool and not nearly as angry as she'd hoped they would be.

Nervously she glanced in his father's direction, but Cecil Barksdale went a lot more gently into the night than his son. His eyes were blurred and stricken as if Aaron had somehow hurt him. Impossible.

"I want to go home," she said, because she felt slightly sick, and she didn't want to spend the evening with witty, charming Aaron and his bastard of a father.

"As you wish," he said, and they left the party with only the smallest of goodbyes.

Thank God.

AARON TOOK HER BACK to the Four Seasons. He didn't want to assume, but he wasn't going to ask. He needed to hold her tonight. He needed to be with her tonight, he wanted to erase the memory of his father's behavior.

Her skin was pale and chilled and he ran a tubful of hot water, undressing her carefully, because he owed her this.

"I'm sorry," he said, sitting at the edge of the tub, watching as she slid down into the water. It wasn't the moment to feel a hard punch of lust. He should be concerned and worried, and wanting to take care of her.

"Your father is a jerk."

"*Bastard* is the better word," he corrected, noting the exhausted smile on her face as she let the water lap over her, bare nipples riding above the surface. Her thighs parted, not in invitation but in languor, but it didn't matter. His cock swelled and ached just the same.

"Did you know he would be there?" she asked, and he put his hands on her shoulders, rubbing the tight muscles because he wanted to touch her, and her sigh was pure bliss.

"He never leaves. My paternal doppelgänger."

She covered his hand with one of her own. "I'm sorry."

For long torturous minutes, he rubbed her shoulders, not allowing his fingers to steal lower. Comfort, he reminded himself. When the water turned cool, he handed her the towel and dried her off, lingering only slightly.

When he turned out the lights, she curled into his arms and promptly fell asleep, and he pressed a gentle kiss to her hair. Alone in the dark, his cock pulsed like some selfish heart, but being alone was no less than he deserved.

Bastard.

ACCORDING TO THE HISTORY books, the Spanish Inquisition had ended a few hundred years earlier, but Jenn knew the feeling. The summons had been hand-delivered to her apartment. Lunch with Didi Ziegler. Alone.

In lieu of chain mail and bulletproof vests, Jenn opted for unassuming white linen, accessorized with yellow polka-dotted sandals and a confident smile.

They met for sushi, and Jenn eyed the remains of the sliced fish on her plate with a sinking sensation. There was pointless chitchat until the waiter cleared the dishes, and then Didi moved in for the kill.

"In this town, there are very few secrets. I kept expecting you to disappear, but you have not, which makes me reassess my earlier opinion of you. I do not like reassessing the world. Time is too precious, especially for a woman of my advanced years. I've had you vetted for my own peace of mind, but a few pertinent facts and a meandering life do not tell me your heart. So, what are your intentions?"

"I sleep with him. That's the extent of it."

"I see. Very cosmopolitan." She shrugged it off. "At least he tells me that he is writing again. That's something."

"He never stopped," Jenn said, needing to get the record straight. The world thought Aaron Barksdale had frozen under the pressure of fame. The truth was, Aaron had merely relocated his world to someplace else where he could be comfortable and write in peace. It surprised her that Didi didn't know this. Aaron would never stop writing. Heck, he would stop breathing first.

"You know this for sure?"

"He's got twenty manuscripts under his bed."

Didi slapped a hand on the table and the crystal jumped. Literally. "And he did not show them to me? Oh, the cad! I could have retired by now. I could be sunning myself on a beach in the Rivera, but instead he hoards all his little pages like a feral rodent." She pushed up her lenses, the better to stare sternly at Jennifer. "He's told you this, or did you use your journalistic skills to discover it?"

"You don't like reporters, either?" Jenn guessed, using her skills with great success.

"A bit-time reviewer trashed his book. Aaron drank for months."

"I didn't know about the drinking," she murmured, wishing she could go back in time and erase so much of his pain, but she couldn't, and apparently he'd beaten some of his demons on his own. The drinking explained the differences between the page-ripping exploits of Aaron Barksdale, author vivant, and Aaron Barksdale the man.

Didi waved a careless hand. "You wouldn't know, no one cared. The world sees the writer as a tormented soul. They never believe that it is the world that is the tormentor. But you want to be a writer, as well?"

"I'm a journalist, not a writer."

"And how is your career going?"

"You know how my career is going," stated Jennifer, not quite a guess.

"He is looking out for you. You turned down the job at the *Long Island Herald?*"

"You know about that, too?"

"Darling, where do you think the offer came from?"

"I see," she said, wishing her fairy godmother had opted to tell her.

"At Aaron's insistence. I told him he should let you toil in your drudgery, but he wouldn't. Does it bother you, his wanting to take care of you? Some women would rebuff such advantages, some would take advantage of it. Of him."

"I'm a good journalist," Jenn stated, picking her words carefully. "It's a very hard field. If someone opens a door,

I won't turn it down, but I don't need it. I'm good enough to get back to the *Times* on my own," she stated. And it was true. After so long doubting herself, she realized that she was in this for the long haul. No matter the drudgery.

"The *Times?*"

"My previous employer," Jenn told her, possibly bragging.

"That is very prestigious."

"Yes," Jennifer answered, tucking a strand of hair behind her ear.

"You think he will help you return to the fold?"

"I don't need Aaron for that. What I want from Aaron is to be with him."

Didi looked over Jennifer, seeing the flaws, but seeing her heart, too. Finally she nodded with approval. "I like you. You're very Alphabet City. I don't like Alphabet City, but we all have our imperfections. He will need someone soon. I have always been the center of his universe, but I am closing my agency, and he will hurt. He will need you. You are up to this task?"

"He doesn't know you're retiring," Jenn stated, because the news would kill him. There were few people in the world that Aaron cared for. Didi was pretty much it. And now Jenn. Maybe. Probably. Okay. Definitely.

"I told him about my leaving the business. He believed I was joking. Perhaps I did not tell him in such an unaffected way, but I dislike sincerity. Eventually we will talk. He should know the truth. He will need to prepare. Aaron must depart that cesspool of small-town Americana—he has lived there too long. I have been soft, spoiling him like a favored pet, letting him sulk out in the wilds with their simple smiles and their meat in a can. You cannot hurt him, I will not let you. I come from a long line of Romanians.

Very cruel with long memories. I'm sure you've heard about our curses."

"I thought you were German."

"A German Rom," clarified Didi. "But my heritage is not my concern. He is."

"No one could hurt Aaron," clarified Jennifer.

"His father nearly killed him, just as he drove Aaron's mother to the grave."

"His father is a bastard," she stated firmly.

"Yes, and Aaron believes that the apple must not fall far from the tree. It didn't help that Cecil knew where to strike. The public flogging in *The Paris Review?* That was his father."

Oh, my. Jennifer had read that review. *Intellectual shenanigans, disguised as art. A meandering maundering of monumental proportions.* And those were the nice things.

"I thought John O'Connell reviewed the book."

"His father's pen name, not that he ever used it. Except for the one time. He hates Aaron's success. Aaron is Van Gogh to Cecil's kindergarten handprints. He is Beethoven to Cecil's karaoke. Aaron was the Bard of Brooklyn. He could be again."

It was no wonder that Aaron had such an inflated sense of ego if his agent was always buttering him up like that. Of course it was the truth, but did everyone have to keep pointing that out? "His writing isn't that good," Jenn quibbled with a disdainful sniff.

Didi started to smile. "Did you tell him that?"

"Absolutely."

"You lied merely to prick his overripe ego?"

"Possibly. No. Definitely," corrected Jennifer.

"Good. I like you very much. If you hurt him, I will kill you. At one time, I had a lover, an Italian prince, who gave me a jeweled knife that belonged to his ancestors. I still have it. It's very elegant, very deadly. It can disembowel you and slice your innards like a Japanese eel's. In the end I had to dump him, poor man. He was much too much in love. Men can be such fools when they're in love. They become tedious."

Jenn understood the warning, she respected the warning, but it wasn't necessary. It wasn't within Jenn's power to hurt Aaron. The man could withstand a nuclear blast without wincing. If there was anybody who was going to end up heartbroken and tedious, it was Jenn.

"Do you need something from me?" she asked, mainly to be polite.

"I need many things. An eunuch that will fall on my every word, the complete demise of the Internet and the proper respect for the principles of Marxism, but these dreams are impossible, so I must endure. Come along," she commanded, snapping her fingers as if Jenn was her pet. "The waiter will think we are friends."

Jenn trailed after her, with the beginnings of a smile. "No. We mustn't have that."

THERE WERE EXPECTATIONS in this thing called a relationship. There were schedules and assumed plans and a certain amount of time required to be spent together, and not all could be sex. Slowly Aaron eased his way back into a world that he'd left. It wasn't easy, but Jennifer was easy, not in the sexually promiscuous way, although she was fairly forward thinking, a fact that he appreciated, but she was easy company. She was learning to judge his moods and knew when to press, and when he needed her to sink down in his lap and love him.

He rented the apartment above her, but hadn't made his way to informing her of this fact. The constant train rides were now a pain in the ass, and he found that he could write as well in an apartment as he could in the cabin in the woods. There weren't many furnishings in his new lodgings. A bed, the equipment to prepare food for Two, his typewriter and his gas lamp.

His relationship with Kevin was progressing in a backward manner. Each time he saw the boy, Kevin only resented him more. Jennifer would ask about Kevin, but Aaron knew that she expected him to report on these disastrous meetings, and sometimes he would tell her the truth, but sometimes he spun a work of fiction, implying that Aaron and Kevin were starting to bond.

Maybe she suspected the truth; he wasn't quite sure. His writing had changed, his way of looking at the world was changed, glowing from her light, but he didn't tell her that, either.

It was her writing that worried him. She sold articles to some low-rent publications on the world of Dumpster diving, on the chess clubs in Harlem and on the new baby penguins at the Bronx Zoo, but they were beneath her. She'd received a job offer from a weekly in Paramus, but she turned it down, which bothered him because he knew why she turned it down. She wanted to write for the *Times*. At one point, she had written for the *Times*, but she'd lost her job because of him. She didn't say these words. She didn't even blame him for it, which she should have, but Aaron knew he was responsible. He'd asked Didi to work her connections there, but first-rate newspaper jobs did not grow on trees, and nothing came of it, which bothered him more.

So, when she suggested they go out to dinner with her parents, he jumped at the idea, even though he hadn't the foggiest notion of how a traditional Meet-the-Parents scenario was supposed to unfold.

They met at Eleven Madison, and Henry and Marian Dade were not the ogres he feared. Frankly they were very nice people, a little older than he expected. They were in their late sixties, and it was apparent they doted on their only child. Marian Dade was a doctor at Cornell Medical Center, currently contemplating retirement, and Henry Dade was a vice president at a bank.

The dinner was a tense, silent affair, with Jennifer's parents not asking about her employment nor their relationship. When they asked about him, Jennifer would deflect their questions with the patient yet ineffectual kindness most often seen from a playschool teacher.

"So how did you two meet?" asked Dr. Dade.

"At a library," answered Jennifer, but Aaron stepped in.

"I live in Harmony Springs, where Jennifer was earlier in the summer."

"You must not see each other very often. That's such a long way."

"I take the train into the city every few days."

"That must get expensive. What did you say you do? I don't remember what Jennifer told us."

"I didn't tell you, Mother."

"I'm a writer."

"Oh," chimed in her father, not an encouraging sound.

Jennifer looked at him in surprise, and he shrugged.

"Do you ever think of moving to the city? I suppose you couldn't afford it. Everything is so expensive. We've been trying to get Jennifer into steadier employment, but she seems determined to follow her dreams, no matter how improbable."

"She's very talented. She'll be fine."

"I suppose. But I would sleep easier if she could settle down. Have you ever thought about a real job?" her mother asked him, smiling at him with those warm brown eyes that were much like her daughter's.

"Mom!" Jenn protested, but Aaron trudged onward.

"No. It's all right. I didn't go to college, so I don't have a lot of career options."

"So you won't be moving into the city," assumed her mother, whom he expected had already condemned him to a fine career in burger-flipping.

"I might someday," he answered vaguely, deciding it wasn't a good time to mention that he already occupied the apartment above her.

"When you hit it big," muttered her father, drinking from his glass of wine and shooting dark looks in Aaron's direction.

"Maybe then," Aaron agreed.

By the end of the night, Aaron was secretly convinced that they should have told Jennifer's parents he was a drug dealer—they would have been more enthusiastic. He did insist on picking up the check, earning brownie points wherever he could. When he handed the waiter his card, the man looked at his name and gasped.

"Aaron Barksdale? Really?"

At this, Jennifer's father perked up. "He knows you?"

"I had one book published," admitted Aaron, hoping to earn a little more respect.

"And the waiter wants your autograph?" puzzled her father.

"It was a very famous book," stated Jennifer, defending him to the end.

Her father wasn't impressed. "I don't keep up with the book industry. We don't read very much. Journals, newspapers. Real things."

And everyone was a critic.

11

THE SUMMER WAS LONG and hot, and Jenn and Aaron settled into an odd routine of "Let's Pretend." At some point he moved into the apartment above hers, but did the cement-mouthed man choose to inform her of the fact? Oh, no. Instead he headed for the train station…on the *nights they didn't sleep at his hotel.* If the New York tourism industry was booming it was solidly because Aaron was determined to deny the existence of any sort of attachment, emotional, physical, even, alas, geographical. At least the man was consistent.

The job offers from God knows where were flying in with a regularity that should have made the Department of Labor happy. Feeling more and more unsettled, Jenn turned them down, and every Tuesday she walked to the employment office at the *Times.* She wrote articles and sent them off, supplementing her income and keeping her resume intact, but the *Times* was her dream. It was prestige. Her parents would approve of her once again, and she could hold her head high.

Aaron told her that it didn't matter. A fine bit of encouragement from a man who kept his Pulitzer in his underwear drawer.

Contrary to Aaron, every day it grew more difficult for Jenn to keep her mouth shut. Three little words that kept echoing in her brain.

I. Love. You.

She didn't tell him. It seemed wrong on principle. That, and fear that any hint of emotional attachment would send him off screaming. But she kept up hope.

Sometimes he would tell her things. They had dessert at the Gramercy Tavern to celebrate when he finally broke down and gave his manuscripts to Didi—who, by the way, *still* hadn't told Aaron she was retiring.

And Natalie wondered why Jenn was tense? *Secrets*. Too many secrets, all of which Jenn was freaking tired of keeping.

"I bet Didi was over the moon," Jenn told him scarfing down on chocolate-raspberry-fudge cake.

Aaron looked at her and laughed. "Didi? She wanted to know why I held out for so long."

He looked excited, animated, very into the moment, and she was glad to see him like that...coming alive.

"When she's sending them out?" she asked. "I bet you could use the advance by now. The Four Seasons isn't cheap." That was the financially conservative Dade talking, the one her mother had raised. And yes, it was possibly to get him to mention that he was now living in the apartment above her.

"She had four offers on the lot already. Martin wants a preempt, so you don't have to worry. The hotel's safe for a while," Aaron told her, as if she truly was the financially conservative Jennifer Dade that she claimed to be.

"Lovely," answered Jenn, stuffing her mouth with cake so no screams of frustration could emerge.

"It doesn't bother you, does it?"

Really? Slowly Jenn put down her fork, noticing that

he was looking at her concerned, attentive…emotionally bonded. "It bothers me a little. Certainly I know that you feel like you need to withhold things from me…"

His eyes grew puzzled, confused. Still emotionally bonded, but befuddled, as well. "Are we talking about the books?"

He thought she was jealous? Dear God, professional jealousy didn't even rate in the big equation of why Jenn was stressing. "No," she told him, not sure she was ready to have this conversation. Correction. She was plenty ready to have a conversation about their relationship, but Aaron was not.

"What are we talking about?" asked the man who wasn't ready to talk, but sounding suspiciously like a man who *was* ready. Jenn wasn't fooled.

"We're talking about talking. Saying things. Talking about things. Things that make us happy. Things that make us sad. Things we might keep bottled up until we think we're going to bust a valve. A heart valve, by the way."

"Have I done something wrong?" Again, he looked earnestly and sincerely as if he wanted to talk about things, and she told herself not to be the woman who sees things in a man because she wants to see them. Objective thinking, she reminded herself.

"No. You've been perfect." And he had been. Aaron had been playing this relationship straight from the American Boyfriend Handbook.

"Then is something making you sad? Is it the job?"

She sighed. "I don't care about the job. Give me a job. Give me a roof. I'm happy."

Aaron frowned at her, shaking his head. "That's not true. You want to work for the *Times*. You have turned down a lot of offers because you keep telling me that you want to get back at the *Times*," he reminded her.

"I don't know what I want," she lied. "No, that's not true," she corrected herself. "I want to be happy." It was the truth, perhaps not the truthiest of truths, because she wanted him to love her, and she knew that he loved her, but for him to admit that, he would have to first acknowledge the existence of that rare, passion-plumed endangered species known as love.

"I like when you're happy," he told her, which was a nice thought, but not exactly what she wanted to hear.

"What makes you happy?" she asked him, wondering if he ever thought about it, wondering if he ever equated happiness to "them."

He stared at her blankly. "I don't know."

More violently than necessary, Jenn dug into her cake, ignoring the delicate middle and heading straight for the chocolate. "Chocolate. Chocolate makes me happy."

He took away her fork and his smile was nice, sincere... almost understanding. "You. You make me happy."

And then magically, she didn't need her chocolate. She could look into those glimmering eyes, no longer detached, no longer cool, and everything she needed was there. "Aaron?"

"Yes?"

But she couldn't do it. She couldn't say the words because Aaron was not the clueless man that he pretended, and he knew exactly where she was leading, and if he was refusing to follow, it was because he wasn't ready to go there. Not yet. "It's nothing. Let's go home."

"To the Four Seasons?" he asked.

"Sure," she answered, and took a last biteful of chocolate for the road. She was going to need it.

THE SUMMER WAS LONG and hot, July merging into August, and Aaron felt the heavy weight of impossible expectations upon him. Kevin expected a perfect father. Jennifer expected a perfect lover. At least Didi had her perfect book.

Except for his writing, nothing seemed to turn out like the perfection that he desperately wanted. His relationship with Kevin was strained, but with Jennifer, he'd never been happier.

Every day he pretended to take the train into the city, an elaborate charade to keep the truth from her and he wasn't even sure why it was so important to pretend. He waited for the right opportunity to tell her, the right opportunity to tell her how much she meant to him, but he couldn't find the words or more accurately, how to say them. Each time he tried, his throat grew dry and tight, and his head began to hurt, and Jennifer would look at him curiously, as if she knew, but she never delved. The woman with the insatiable curiosity couldn't find the words, either.

After the disastrous meeting with his father, Aaron wisely chose not to attend any more parties. It was better that Jennifer thought he had no friends than to spend time with the people who were.

Although, after he met some of Jennifer's former co-workers, he revised his interpretation of the word *friend*. Slowly he began to understand. Certainly he would still sit quietly while they chatted, talking about nothing, and seeming to enjoy it.

She went on interviews for journalism jobs, but Jennifer, the woman who had set her clocks by her need to be a reporter, had suddenly forgotten it. Or maybe not. One night, when Jennifer had gone off to check a message on her phone, Martina had explained it.

"She's waiting to go back to the *Times*."

He stared deep into the diet cola, stirring at bubbles as if they were the most dreaded poison on the planet. Guilt did that to a man. He could have insured that she kept her job. He *should* have insured that she kept her job. If he truly loved her, he would have done that. But he didn't.

"She could settle for something else in the interim. She's had enough chances," he pointed out and Martina nodded sagely.

"Yes, that would be logical, but then her parents would start lecturing, so she's choosing to wait."

"You're telling me this so I'll feel guilty."

"Of course. I'm a woman. It's what we do best, inflict guilt upon men so that they can shower us with romantic and thoughtful gestures that they forget the other 99.9 percent of the time."

"Very clever."

"It's genetically coded in the DNA."

"What am I supposed to do?" he asked, even though deep down in the hollows of his chest, he knew. He could get her job back for her, and if he truly loved her, he would.

"You can do nothing. Make her happy. You make her happy."

"Are you sure?" He wasn't. In the balance of the relationship equation, he felt like Jennifer gave everything, and Aaron gave all that he could…which was far less than everything. He justified this by telling himself that he had very little of himself left. A writer is a specter on the wall, whose value is defined by how honestly he can observe without bias, without emotion, without a heart. But now those words felt uncomfortably false.

That night, on their way home, he bought Jennifer flowers from a vendor on the street.

"Here. You should have these," he said, pushing them toward her.

"Why are you doing this?"

"Because I should," he answered.

She inhaled and smiled at him in that politely detached way, but he knew he had disappointed her, and he wished he could do things right.

On Labor Day weekend, Didi was having her annual bash at the Hamptons. Lately it seemed like Didi was pressing him to get out more among editors and agents as if he had a book coming out. Which he did, but he wasn't anxious to assume the famous author persona. He liked the man who wrote in the woods, a wise and modest Thoreau rather than an egotistical Nabokov.

The party started out well enough. The day was warm, the sand was soft, and the people were thankfully sober. For a long time he stood, watching Jennifer play chess with Martin and a quiet calm settled over him.

Peace.

It was odd feeling the heat of the sun on his skin, the glaring rays reflecting off the ocean, and the tang of the sea in the air. For a second, only a second, he felt himself feel, let his heart pump something thick and liquid and warm.

His mouth curved upward, and he understood why people craved this like a drug. It colored the world through its prism of color and smudged the sharp edges of absolute truth. It made him feel as happy as a golden glass of Scotch.

No. Happier. The Scotch would numb him.

This. This made him feel.

Jennifer looked at him and smiled and he wondered if he could tell her what she brought to him. The golden glow of life that surrounded her, that had drawn him from the first, leading him further and further into the sticky mire that the world knew as reality.

Before her, he preferred the reality in his mind. The sky

could be any color he chose, the character spouted words that he cherry-picked for their effect, and the feelings that moved him weren't based on anything real, anything that could hurt him. He was the master of all, the conductor that played the music as he wished. But now the skies in his mind weren't quite as soft as the ones in the sky, the currents of the ocean weren't nearly as warm as the one that lay outstretched before him, and there was no heaven that could compare to a night in her arms.

For a second, he opened his heart, and let the waves of emotions flow through him like water, and he wasn't sure if now that he had opened that door, he was strong enough to close it again.

But maybe it wasn't so awful if it stayed open? Jennifer was safe and warm and golden, and he wanted so desperately to sit and bask in her sun.

"You're looking very happy this afternoon." The voice belonged to Nathan Klein who ran an independent press in Jersey. He was well-respected and bookish in a way that few people were anymore.

Aaron glanced over, nodded once. "I am."

"I suppose when a man has everything, he's entitled to smile."

"I don't have everything," he answered truthfully. "But almost." It was there. He was there. Just within his grasp.

"I don't blame you. It's a good thing you sold off the books before Didi retires."

Aaron knew better than to wade into the quicksand, but he did anyway because he was feeling too happy, too blindly revisionist, too foolish to do otherwise. "She's not going to leave me."

A dark flush ran up Nathan's face, the sort of flush that spoke of embarrassment, of words spoken out of turn, of truths laid bare before their time. "You didn't know?"

The sun burned on Aaron's skin, baking him there like a fried egg on the pavement. He could feel a bead of sweat slide down his back, slow and torturous. Jennifer looked over, and began to walk toward him.

Aaron, who never reacted in public, walked away.

She caught up with him as he was striding toward the main highway. He wasn't sure of his destination, but walking seemed the appropriate response.

"What happened? What did he say?" She grabbed his arm, trying to stop him, but he didn't think anyone could stop him right now.

"Nathan was lying to me," Aaron insisted, trying to wrest back control when he had none. "He said Didi was going to retire."

Jennifer stopped, and the flash of light around her was too much. "He wasn't lying, Aaron."

At that, Aaron shut his eyes, blocking her out, because there comes a time when you can no longer look into the sun without going blind. "How do you know?"

"Didi told me."

Realizing he could not shut her out forever, Aaron opened his eyes, blinking, trying to restore his perception back to its normal, placid state, but there was a golden fog in front of his eyes, in front of his mind. There were those damned shards in his heart, and he wanted them out. "Why didn't you tell me?" he asked, his voice cool and detached.

"I'm sorry," she told him, and he could see the guilt in her eyes, and the pain that she felt for him.

"If you knew this, why didn't you tell me?"

"I wanted to, but I couldn't. It wasn't my place," she lied, and he knew she was lying because she knew it was her place. He knew it was her place. And Jennifer, the woman who had never been unable to express herself, the woman who put her heart out on the table for anyone who wanted to feast upon it, was suddenly making excuses for not telling him the truth.

"Then whose place is it? The newspapers', my father's, some stranger's on the street?" His voice was growing louder, a marvelous imitation of a man in a high fit of rage, and he wanted her to hurt as badly as he did. Aaron had never liked to hurt, and she had almost convinced him that he wouldn't have to hurt anymore, but that, like so much of her world, was a lie. A big fat lie, and it was one that he almost believed…because he loved her.

12

JENNIFER HAD NEVER seen him angry, never seen his eyes blaze as if they were lit from within, and right now those blazes were directed at her—the innocent bystander, the plucky cheerleader, the woman who had known exactly who much this was going to hurt.

Damn Didi for making Jenn do the dirty work.

"I know this hurts. I'm sorry," she offered, wishing that there were better words, some magic formula to make him whole.

"I trusted you," he yelled, his hands balled into fists, and he stood there, with the ocean in the distance, the holiday traffic buzzing by, and yelled at her about trust.

Calmly she kept her eyes focused on the road, the sparkles of the sand, anything but the rage in his eyes. He was hurt, lashing out at whatever was near. She couldn't take this personally. "I'm not the one who betrayed your trust," she pointed out quite logically. "You need to take this up with Didi."

"I don't care about Didi. This is about you. We don't have secrets, Jennifer. I thought you knew that. I thought you were honest with me."

We don't have secrets? It was at that point that she lost

some of the rational calmness, because she had spent the entire summer telling herself that he needed space and time to grow. Time to trust her. But now? Oh, no, now she was the villain in the piece, the one who was the roadblock on the great relationship in his life—the one that he wanted all along? It was at that point that she got into his face and jabbed a finger into his chest.

"Trusted me? You've been living in the apartment above me and you haven't bothered to let me in on that little secret. You didn't tell me your real name until you didn't think you would see me again. If you want honesty, if you want that sort of communication, you have to open yourself up to it."

He grew quiet, his eyes cooler, and she knew the thought processes were starting up again. "How long have you known?"

Jenn waited, not wanting to answer this.

"How long?" he repeated, wanting her to answer this.

"Since July," she muttered, digging her sandals into the sand, wishing it was her head.

"You should have told me."

"Didi should have told you," she insisted.

"Didi isn't you," he said, and she knew why he was mad at her. She even understood why he felt betrayed. But betrayal involves attachment, involves commitment, involves emotions and dammit, if she was going to go down for this one, she was going to have earned it. She wanted him to say it. She wanted him to see why it mattered.

"Why is that so important, Aaron? Why am I different? Or is this just another 'let's blame it on the world' vendetta, where the entire apocalypse falls down on Aaron, who is left to wander the trials of civilization alone. You want the world that fits in with your misogynistic ways because it's easier than having to love and feel and hurt. I'm sorry your father was a bastard, but he was, and that ship has sailed. Everything now is just on you."

"You don't like me very much, do you?" he asked quietly.

"I love you."

There. It was out. He didn't want secrets? Ha. No secrets anymore. Carefully she looked at him, looked to the very heart of him, waiting for him to respond in kind.

"That's no answer to the question I asked," he told her, but it was an answer to the unspoken question that she had asked.

Do you love me?

I won't admit it.

"That's all you're going to say?" she asked, giving him another chance, praying desperately that he could do this.

He stuffed his hands into his jeans and met her eyes, and she could see the nerves there, see all the old scars bubbling above the surface. "What do you want from me?"

"You love me, Aaron. Why don't you admit it?"

Stubbornly he shook his head. "I don't."

"You're lying."

"No," he told her, lying to the end, and Jenn quit trying to heal a shipwrecked heart. She couldn't take the pain.

She wiped at her eyes, furious at the tears, furious that he could sit there calm, composed, and she needed to fall apart, but maybe that had been the problem all along.

"I thought you were better than this. I thought you wanted to be better than this, but apparently I was deluding myself just like you said. Imagine that. For once you were right. Get out of my life, Aaron, because I deserve someone better than that."

INSTEAD OF LISTENING TO lectures from Natalie, or indulging in a multitude of vices with Martina, Jenn chose to go home. Not to her apartment, but to her parents'. Yes, there would be lectures, but she needed to hear them. She needed to have her mother's words ringing in her ears so that she could summon up relief rather than pain.

When she came through the door, her mother knew something was wrong, and she didn't give her lectures. Not this time. Instead she folded her up in her arms and held her, and for a long time Jennifer cried, because it was one thing to be unloved by Aaron Barksdale, but it was another, more painful thing to know that he loved you, but would never, ever know it.

AARON STARTED AT A BAR. He ordered a glass of Red Label. Neat. And he almost drank from the well. He wanted something to restore his equilibrium. Something that would keep all the emotions at bay. But alcohol wasn't it.

In the end, he packed up his cat and his typewriter, and took the train back to Harmony Springs.

There was only one thing to keep him sane.

His writing.

13

IT WAS ANOTHER THREE weeks before she heard the sounds of a typewriter being misused from the apartment above her. It surprised her because she thought that Aaron would not come back, and she had taught her heart how not to hurt so much. Not really. The pain was still there, the knowledge that he didn't want the sort of happy life dreams that she did. But there were the sounds of his writing, the sounds of one typewriter, suffering under the fiery whiplash of his hands. She tried not to smile. She told herself not to race upstairs, that he would come see her when he was ready. Possibly another three weeks, and she listened to the music of his work, the carnival calliope of the tap-tap-tap-tap-tap-tap-ding, and she let herself smile.

Maybe.

It took him seven days before he knocked on her door. Natalie answered, looked at Jenn—who had gained seven pounds after the breakup—with concern, but Jenn knew it would be okay. He took her hand and took her upstairs, and opened the door to his apartment, and let her inside.

It was large and sparsely furnished and would need serious decorator attention, but it wasn't the place that drew her. It was the man.

Wisely she crossed her arms over her chest, her mouth cemented shut, and waited for him to speak. Eventually he did.

"I couldn't stay away from you. I thought about drinking. Thought that if drowned myself in a river of Scotch, I could forget you. But I knew it wouldn't be enough. There's not enough Scotch in the world to do that. There's nothing that could make me forget you. Even if you wrote that article, even if you destroyed me, I'd still want you. I'd still dream of you. I hate myself for that. I want to hate you, but I can't. I want to blame you for everything that hurts me. I want to block you from my mind, but I can't." He looked pale, his eyes red-rimmed and fierce, glowing like embers in his face. "Why do you stay with me?"

She uncrossed her arms, uncemented her mouth, and unlocked her heart. He could do that so easily. "You don't know, do you? It's not even in your realm of consciousness that someone could love you."

"I'm a vile person, and I don't play well with others," he answered without a shred of doubt, and it surprised her that he could be so unaware.

The vile cat mewed from the top of the refrigerator, probably to tell Aaron that he was wrong. "You have a heart the size of the Matterhorn. It is icy and slippery and a person could die from it, but it's there. And it's very big."

He still looked at her skeptically, but she could see that icy heart melting in his eyes. "How can you love me?"

Aaron seemed to have problems with that concept, the idea that he could be loved. And perhaps that explained his disbelief in love. He'd grown up without the love of his father, with only a ghost of his mother. The people who were supposed to love him never did. To a child's mind, it was better that love didn't exist than to believe there was something unloveable within them.

Finally she walked to him and put a hand on his chest, feeling the erratic beat, the tense rhythms within him. "You have a large heart and you do great things for other people, growling and snapping the whole time, as if it makes you miserable."

"It does make me miserable," he insisted, stubborn to the core.

"Is it so hard to be loved, Aaron?" she whispered.

He stroked her hair, cupping her cheek. "I like it better when you yell at me and call me names. And then all I can think about is ripping off your clothes. Getting you naked."

"Then I think we'll always have to fight," she told him, locking her hands over his, keeping him there.

"You'll always be with me?"

"As long as you need me," she promised.

"That'll be forever."

That night Jennifer slept in his arms, and in the darkest part of night, in the darkest corner of his mind, Aaron knew he loved her, and his love wasn't the nice sort that you would ever read in a gilt book of poems. It was a violent and selfish beast that skulked through the world with dark claws and the fires of pain in its eyes. He would destroy any man who hurt her, who touched her, who dared tried to steal her away, because she was his and his alone. He didn't understand why her eyes looked on him with that miraculous softness. He didn't understand why one moment she would curse him and the next she could stroke his hair. He didn't understand these things—they puzzled him. They worried him.

But he knew he would die if she ever stopped.

THE NEXT DAY WAS TUESDAY, the September sun was spitting mad, and he met Didi in the lobby of the *New York*

Times. She was dressed in her best red suit. The one that didn't show blood.

"You love her."

"Yes," he admitted, because Didi knew him, she knew what he was and what he wasn't. She didn't expect him to be good and noble and selfless and all those other things that were considered admirable. Jenn saw him through her love-struck glasses, but she was determined to wear them, and he prayed that she'd never take them off.

"This terrifies you?"

"*Eviscerate* is the more accurate word. Perhaps *exsanguinate,* leeching all the blood and human life from my body. She carries my heart, my soul, and she leads my cock on a short chain."

"That is good. That is the love that will last. And does she love you? What am I saying? Of course she does. She lives with you, subjects herself to the lash of your tongue, endures the tsunami of your ego. It's either love or dementia, and she seems very sound."

"You like her?" That was the thing. Jenn was so very likeable. She was nice and funny and people liked being near her. But he didn't worry what the rest of the world thought, only Didi. He needed Didi to like her. He needed Didi to approve, because he had done very few good things in his life. Actually there was only one. Jenn was his first. Barring a partial lobotomy, or a personality-altering brain injury, she would most likely be his last.

Didi laughed at him, but not in a bad way. "What does my opinion matter? You will do as you will. If I said I hated her, would you leave her? No. If I said I liked her, would you marry her? No. I am merely a fastidious old woman who wants to live a life of leisure without the pain and agony of dealing with responsibility."

"We'll go to France."

"Why would we want to go to France? There are French people there, with their French ways and their French food. As if they are the center of the world."

"The Caribbean? Warm beach, turquoise waters the exact color of the curtains at Le Cirque?"

"Please. It is like being transported to the Dark Ages. Have you listened to the endless singing, and besides, I'm allergic to coconut."

"We should do something together. A vacation. I want you to know Jenn. I want you to love her. I want to make you happy. I haven't done that enough." It was a shameless bribe because he wanted to keep Didi in his life. If she wasn't his agent, maybe she would be his friend.

"I cannot be happy. You are not a man for vacation. We must embrace who we are honestly, without vapid sentimentality."

"I could be a man for vacation. People do that. They talk and live together. They watch television in dark rooms without talking or seething in quiet misery. We'll take a vacation. Where do you want to go? Anywhere."

"Anywhere?"

"Anywhere. Prague. The Alps. Paris. You love French cuisine."

"It gives me heartburn. I shall stay in New York. And perhaps I will take up skydiving or learn to knit. If you want to take me somewhere, then we'll dine at Michaels so that people can see I'm not wheezing at death's door. Already they are calling with their quiet questioning voice. Asking how are things as if I can't peer into their dark and greedy hearts. They are waiting for me to leave this business so that they can court you and woo you and seduce you with their promiscuous agenting ways. You must be smart. You must choose wisely. Lawrence Price is good. John Beck will be fair, but he will not coddle you, and it

will make you angry. Then you will kill him, and do you
know the first that the courts throw the book at? The writers. Clarissa Spencer is a well-trained puppy who will roll
over at the first sign of trouble. You will always be trouble.
Clarissa would be bad."

The receptionist in the lobby walked over, her smile
polite and untouchable.

"Mr. Barksdale? Ms. Ziegler? Mr. Kingsley will see you
now."

Together they walked upstairs, and Aaron reminded
himself that he wasn't nervous, but it surprised him that he
wasn't. This was going to be right. He was going to make
it right.

The office was nearly overflowing with paper, newspapers, magazines and books, and Quinn Kingsley, the
man who had laid off Jennifer, looked at both of them and
smiled quickly, the trademarked expression of a man who
lives his life on a deadline.

Aaron respected the whip of the deadline and got right
down to business.

"I never liked this paper. You're a group of political
hacks who couldn't investigate your own asses because
the stench would offend the sensibilities. I don't know why
Jennifer would choose to write here, but she does. You'll
hire her back now. She won't know of this meeting. If she
does, I'll make sure you wife knows about the hot little
number at the city desk and the used condom in your trash.
In return for Jenn's continued employment, you get me and
my books. An exclusive peek at the books. An exclusive on
my life. The good. The bad. The things that people don't
know and always whispered about when they thought I
couldn't hear. It will be raw and unflinching, and your
readers will be thrilled with my own downfall."

"Why didn't you write an autobiography?" asked Quinn,

clearly intrigued, but not willing to commit. Not yet. Aaron knew the type.

"Autobiographies should not be a cautionary tale. They're about war heroes or presidents. People whose life is worth the price of a hardcover. I don't want to make money from all the mistakes that I've made. I only want Jennifer to have her job back."

Didi, who never smoked, lit up a cigarette as she sat down, took a long drag and then put it out on his desk. Quinn's eyes narrowed, but he refrained from cleaning up the mess. Aaron noticed the overflowing trash can and realized that restraint didn't spill over into all the areas of his life. It was exactly as Jennifer said, and Aaron smiled his crocodile smile.

Quinn picked up a pen and pretended to take notes. "What's the pub date?"

"April," answered Didi. "You'll run the piece a month before the book is out."

"What if the book is crap?" he asked, and Didi gasped, but Aaron stepped in to answer.

"Your paper has descended into crap, people still buy it. Oh. They don't. No matter, my book is not crap."

"Let me think about it," the man quibbled as if he suddenly had all the time in the world.

Then Didi snapped her fingers, and rose to leave. "This is tedious. You make us beg as if we were the downtrodden serfs. We will go to Los Angeles. I yearn for the sun, the air, the people who know when to fawn and bow. The *Times* will not be so bold. Or *People* magazine, although I don't know that I want to see your picture on some drugstore rack, beside the World's Sexiest Man. Do you like Oprah, Aaron? Perhaps Oprah. I do not know. She should have more style, don't you think? All that wealth, and she dresses like a Frau."

Aaron followed her, heading for the door.

Three.

Two.

One.

"Wait."

Didi didn't stop. "Open the door, dahling. Did you hear a voice? I don't think that was a voice. I heard no apology. Perhaps it was a hunger-induced psychosis, hearing tiny voices that do not exist. So, where should we go for lunch? I'm thinking skewered quail, smothered in a tasty oyster cream sauce. Something to make my taste buds sing."

"I'm sorry. Of course we'd love to have the first look at Mr. Barksdale's book."

Didi turned and smiled, showing great teeth, and ten minutes later, the negotiations were done.

"Do you know I love you, Didi?" he told her, practicing as they walked out the glass door of the building, into the bustle of the streets, the noise, the chaos, the life that was New York. Aaron began to smile.

"You are growing soft and maudlin. I am starting to feel old, and you feel the need to spout pithy platitudes that are designed to make me feel comfortable before my retirement. We will discuss it no longer."

That said, she knocked aside a suit and stole the nearest cab. Aaron shrugged at the man apologetically, but it was the evolution of the city. Only the strong survive.

Like Jenn.

Like Aaron.

This time he grinned. Definitely grinned.

14

"It wasn't supposed to end this way. The world was supposed to implode upon itself, a punishment for the sins that the firmament had been forced to endure. The sky had been expected to glow black and empty. The seers had told of seas rising to great heights, a giant mouth to swallow mankind and destroy the poison forever.

"Cain emerged from the hollow in the ground, and was surprised by the sun, by the fiery yellow ball that still hung in the sky, and his skin was warm under its blanket of light."

Aaron sat back in his chair and frowned, ready to rip out the paper and start anew, but he kept rereading the words, and deep in his gut, that merciless critic that never sat silent, the critic...*liked it?*

Who was he fooling? It blew great chunks of sugary cheese, coating his fictional world in a pink cobweb of Utopian joy. Ew.

Yet like the car wreck with the mangled bodies and the screams of agonized pain, he couldn't look away.

That couldn't be right.

Thankfully, before he was forced to endure further literary analysis of the destruction of his creative brain, he heard the knock at the door, checked his watch, and realized that Jennifer had left work early. He pushed at the typewriter and winked at Two, who only stared back blindly.

Two was still loyal to the code of discontent, but Aaron was slowly, joyfully abandoning it.

Jenn walked in, her mouth pulled into that nervous line that never meant good, and he steeled himself for pain.

"I turned down the job this morning," she told him, and he nodded stupidly. It was done. They were over. He had given her the last thing that he could, and she had turned it down.

THE END.

He walked to the typewriter, pulled out the sheet of shit and tore it into long strips that he tossed to the floor like a losing lottery ticket. "Okay, if that's what you want to do."

"I changed my mind," she began to explain, and he held up his hand, because he didn't need to hear anymore.

"Whatever you need to do is fine," he told her, but she chose to ignore his words and carried on, and he realized he was going to have to stand here and listen, when all he wanted to do was run.

"I talked to my mom. I told her that it was time that I didn't worry so much about security, that I didn't worry about appearances. I wanted to be happy. The thought of working at the *Times* doesn't make me happy anymore."

"I shouldn't have done it. I'm sorry."

She walked to him and touched him, and he wished she wouldn't touch him right now because it made him soft and pliable and...hopeful. "It was lovely what you did, but I don't want a bought job."

"*Extortion* is probably the better word," he said, beginning to breathe again because apparently she wasn't breaking up with him—she'd only turned down the job at the *Times*. He stared at the trash on the floor, and wondered if he could piece it back together.

"I'm going to freelance for a while. I'm going to work at Starbucks for a while. I'm going to be happy for a while."

"I can support you."

"Yes, you could support two hundred of me, but I don't need your money nor do I want your money."

"Except for desserts?"

She laughed then, and it was musical, like what heaven must be. "Except for that. I wanted to tell you. I didn't want you to think the wrong thing."

"I wouldn't do that," he lied, and watched her walk toward the door.

She turned and smiled at him. "I love you." Then she turned again, ready to leave, not expecting anything from him at all.

Aaron swallowed the stone in his throat. "I love you, too."

She stopped, but didn't look at him, not yet. She was disbelieving the words, her brain hearing the foreign sound, running on the synanpses of the brain that had not been formed. Until now. He understood that disbelief, that self-doubt, but Jenn was much smarter than he was. Much stronger.

She did turn, and there were tears glimmering in her eyes like diamonds, and he knew he'd done well.

"I've loved you for such a long time. Every day that I write, when I wallow in the most vile and putrid parts of humanity, I make myself keep one light burning. A marker, because without that one flame of brightness, there is no soul, there is no story, there is no man that is worth being born. Sometimes I wake up, surrounded by the dark, drowning in it, but then I hear you breathe, your hair brushes my chest, and I see my candle. I see my soul. It's you. I thought about telling you, but I didn't think you'd believe me, so I waited. And then, I didn't want to tell you, because I'm not good at this. I'm not a good person, and you'd think I was lying, only saying it to keep you happy, so I tried to figure out a way to prove it to you, but there was nothing. Nothing seemed good enough. I don't know what I can do to make you believe, but I'll spend the rest of my life trying."

"I believe you," she told him quietly.

"I don't understand why you don't love someone better than me. Someone easier. Someone who doesn't need a candle to remind them of their soul."

Jenn thought carefully, aware that there were few words that could sway the tormented jihad of this man's heart. "Is there any man who could love me more than you?"

He knew the answer right away. "No. That's the only reason I can live with myself. I should feel guilty that I want to keep you. I should send you away to be with someone who's less of a bastard, but the delicious irony is that I'm too much of a bastard to do that. I couldn't live without you, Jennifer."

He stood stiff, frozen, always expecting her to leave him, and she wasn't sure that the fear would ever go away, and so she walked toward him, and locked her arms around him, mooring them together. Shipwrecked heart? Ha. The shipwrecked heart had finally come home.

Epilogue

December 24

THE RITUALS OF THE holiday season were new to Aaron. His father had never believed in another god apart from his own self-worship, and Two had never bought into the crass commercialism that was the Christmas season. Unlike Jennifer, who, no surprise, was a total sap.

He was giving Kevin an iPhone, and explained that he bought one for himself, as well.

"You aren't supposed to buy your own Christmas presents."

"As you get older, you learn to make exceptions. Sometimes it's easier just to go out and buy something than to explain to someone else how you might have made incorrect assumptions about the use of technology and the hazards of overuse. And this way, by not having to explain all that... It's just easier." He held out the box. "So here."

"You wrapped it, too?"

"The store did it."

"You didn't have to tell me beforehand. You could have let me open it."

Aaron sighed, because in many ways Kevin was as

critical as Aaron. "Next year we'll progress to opening presents and cute surprises and fuzzy puppies and unicorns with rainbows coming out of their asses."

Kevin snickered, and they shared a moment of bonding. Jennifer would be proud.

Sometimes biology bound people together, and sometimes it was something else—the heart. He looked at the boy who wasn't his son and smiled. Someday he wanted a son just like him. "There's a lot of cool things you can do with the phone," he explained. "You can watch movies—do you like to watch movies?"

"Not really."

Aaron beamed proudly. "Excellent. You can also use it as an educational tool."

"Can I download porn?"

"Kevin," he warned, in a stern parental tone, or what he hoped was a stern parental tone.

"I had to ask. Mom doesn't want to talk about that sort of thing."

"Yes, I can see why," Aaron said, and then cleared his throat, because he didn't want to talk about that thing, either. Not yet. Not ever.

"So I can ask you about sex?"

"Not yet. I need some time to work up to the next level. I just got a phone, Kevin."

"Sorry." The boy looked at the phone in his hand, and pushed at the wire frame of his glasses. "Thanks for it. It's pretty cool."

"S'all right."

Aaron got up from the stoop, and Kevin looked at him, almost anxiously. "You'll be here tomorrow."

"After lunch. Your mother said it was okay."

Kevin's smile was awkward and nervous, and Aaron nodded, awkward and nervous, but they both understood.

After leaving the house, he headed for the F train, back to Manhattan, back to Jennifer, back home. He looked at his phone, took a deep breath and punched in her number.

"Hello, Jennifer. It's me."

"Why does caller ID say Aaron Barksdale?"

"It's my cell phone."

There was a loud squeal, heard in five counties, nearly deafening him. Bravely he endured. "What brand?" she asked.

"I don't know," he lied, not wanting to hear her squeal again, at least until he discovered the volume.

"You're becoming a lemming. I hear it in your voice. When I get home, we'll have to watch TV. A reality show. Oh, this is awesome."

"I don't want to watch TV."

"You have other ideas?"

"There's always Scrabble," he suggested.

"You know there are games for the phone…."

Aaron blinked at the photo that had appeared. *Jennifer?* "Did you just send me porn?"

"It's me," she said, and then laughed, low and husky, and Aaron realized that perhaps he was going to like this technology thing after all.

* * * * *

Kay Young returned to woozy consciousness to find that she was lying on a soft sofa beneath a heap of quilts near a cheerfully burning fire. When she tried to move, however, everything hurt, and she groaned.

At once she heard a sound, then a stranger with a hard, harsh face was squatting beside her. "Shh," he said softly. "You're safe here. I promise."

"I have to go," she said weakly, struggling against pain. "He'll find me. He can't find me."

"Easy, lady," he said quietly. "You're hurt. No one's going to find you here."

"He will," she said desperately, terror clutching at her insides. "He always finds me!"

"Easy," he said again. "There's a blizzard outside. No one's getting here tonight, not even the doctor. I know, because I tried."

"Doctor? I don't need a doctor! I've got to get away."

"There's nowhere to go tonight," he said levelly. "And if I thought you could stand, I'd take you to a window and show you."

But even as she tried once more to pull away the quilts, she remembered something else: this man had been gentle when he'd found her beside the road, even when she had kicked and clawed. He hadn't hurt her.

Terror receded just a bit. She looked at him and detected signs of true concern there.

The terror eased another notch and she let her head sag on the pillow. "He always finds me," she whispered.

"Not here. Not tonight. That much I can guarantee."

Will Kay's mysterious rescuer protect her
from her worst fears?
Find out in HER HERO IN HIDING by New York
Times *bestselling author Rachel Lee.*
Available June 2010, only from
Silhouette® Romantic Suspense.

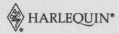

HARLEQUIN®

Showcase

On sale May 11, 2010

Reader favorites from the most talented voices in romance

Save $1.00 on the purchase of 1 or more Harlequin® Showcase books.

SAVE $1.00 on the purchase of 1 or more Harlequin® Showcase books.

Coupon expires Oct 31, 2010. Redeemable at participating retail outlets.
Limit one coupon per purchase. Valid in the U.S.A. and Canada only.

52609015

Canadian Retailers: Harlequin Enterprises Limited will pay the face value of this coupon plus 10.25¢ if submitted by customer for this product only. Any other use constitutes fraud. Coupon is nonassignable. Void if taxed, prohibited or restricted by law. Consumer must pay any government taxes. Void if copied. Nielsen Clearing House ("NCH") customers submit coupons and proof of sales to Harlequin Enterprises Limited, P.O. Box 3000, Saint John, NB E2L 4L3, Canada. Non-NCH retailer—for reimbursement submit coupons and proof of sales directly to Harlequin Enterprises Limited, Retail Marketing Department, 225 Duncan Mill Rd., Don Mills, ON M3B 3K9, Canada.

5 65373 00076 2   (8100)0 11651

U.S. Retailers: Harlequin Enterprises Limited will pay the face value of this coupon plus 8¢ if submitted by customer for this product only. Any other use constitutes fraud. Coupon is nonassignable. Void if taxed, prohibited or restricted by law. Consumer must pay any government taxes. Void if copied. For reimbursement submit coupons and proof of sales directly to Harlequin Enterprises Limited, P.O. Box 880478, El Paso, TX 88588-0478, U.S.A. Cash value 1/100 cents.

HSCCOUP0410

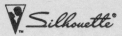

REQUEST YOUR FREE BOOKS!

2 FREE NOVELS PLUS 2 FREE GIFTS!

◈ HARLEQUIN®

Blaze™

Red-hot reads!

HB10R